THE
GO-for-GOLD
GYMNASTS

WITHDRAWN

Winning
TEAM

THE
GO-for-GOLD
GYMNASTS

Winning
TEAM

by DOMINIQUE MOCEANU
and ALICIA THOMPSON

DISNEP • Hyperion Books
New York

Printed in the United States of America
First Edition
10 9 8 7 6 5 4 3 2 1
J689-1817-1-12032

Library of Congress Cataloging-in-Publication Data

Moceanu, Dominique, 1981–
    Winning team / by Dominique Moceanu and Alicia Thompson.—
1st ed.
        p. cm. — (The go-for-gold gymnasts; bk. 1)
    Summary: When twelve-year-old Britt's family moves to Houston so
she can train at an elite gym she looks forward to being part of a team,
but after alienating the other girls and failing to impress her coaches, Britt
begins to figure out what teamwork really means.
        ISBN 978-1-4231-3633-0
    [1. Gymnastics—Fiction. 2. Interpersonal relations—Fiction.
3. Competition (Psychology)—Fiction. 4. Teamwork (Sports)—Fiction.
5. Moving, Household—Fiction. 6. Family life—Texas—Fiction. 7.
Houston (Tex.)—Fiction.] I. Thompson, Alicia, 1984–   II. Title.
    PZ7.M71278Win 2012
    [Fic]—dc23   2011023718

Designed by Tyler Nevins
Text is set in 13 point Minion Pro.
Visit www.disneyhyperionbooks.com

Gymnastics fans past, present, and future,
I dedicate this book to you. Your devotion is
the most essential part of our sport. I have
only the greatest affection for you.
—D.M.

For my sister, Brittany Lee, who inspires me
—A.T.

One

It was late, and my parents and I had been driving through the same state for four hours. I just wanted to go home—well, to my *new* home, which I'd only seen in pictures—but my mom insisted on driving past the gym first.

"After all," she said, turning toward the backseat to smile at me, "it'll practically be your home away from home, right?"

"I guess."

"Aren't you excited? This is such a wonderful opportunity for you." I realized she was waiting for me to smile in return, and so I did, figuring that her neck would probably hurt if she kept her head in that position for too long. Satisfied, she beamed at me and turned back to face the front.

When my parents told me we were moving to Austin, Texas, so I could train with an Elite team, "excited" was certainly not what I felt. It was like everything happened in slow motion—first I heard *moving*, and I thought about everyone I would have to leave behind and my bedroom with the window facing my neighbor's birdbath and the fact that next year for my birthday we were going to play paintball, and I felt sad. Then I heard *Texas*, and I remembered this boy at my gym who used to wear a shirt that said, DON'T MESS WITH TEXAS! in huge letters, and I was scared at the idea of moving to a state that seemed to be all about picking fights for no apparent reason. Ohio doesn't care if you mess with it or not. I mean, obviously it would prefer that you didn't, but if you do, no big deal.

Team, though—that was a little exciting. I used to wish for a teammate. My best friend at my old gym, Dionne, was good, but it would be at least a couple of years before she qualified as Elite, and in the meantime we were split up when it came time to work on specific moves in our routines. With teammates, however, everything would be different. We'd get together in the locker room and say, *Hey, what was up with Coach today? Mood swings much?* At competitions, we'd wear matching French braids and make up silly cheers to spur each other on. During practice, we'd push each other to be better than we'd ever thought possible. I could see it all, running through my head like credits for a sitcom on the Disney Channel as we chalked up the bars for each other and playfully wiped some of the chalk on each other's nose.

When we finally pulled up to the gym, though, it didn't look like the place I'd imagined. For one thing, it was totally deserted. That made sense, considering there aren't too many gymnasts who train at eleven o'clock at night, but it still gave it this really creepy vibe, like it was a ghost town.

"Wow, it's big, huh? Can you believe you'll be training here?" my mom said as my dad parked the truck by the curb. "Come on, let's just take a peek inside."

It wasn't just big. It was *gigantic*. From the outside, it looked like an airplane hangar, or the world's largest indoor flea market or something. Weird, when you think that most of the people who trained there were probably under five feet tall. And when we pressed our faces up against the glass and peered inside, it looked as if it stretched on forever, a wide-open desert with shadows of beams and bars instead of cactuses.

Behind us, I could hear the truck idling as my dad waited for us inside.

I traced the raised letters of the sign on the front door with my fingers: TEXAS TWISTERS: HOME OF STATE BEAM CHAMPION NOELLE ONESTI!

Back in Ohio, my gym had been attached to the Aquatic Center. People would walk into the reception area and go, "Wait a sec, those are *leotards,* not bathing suits. . . ." and then the receptionist would explain that, yeah, the big building wasn't just an indoor pool, it actually had a whole separate gymnastics facility as well. When I made the Elite team, months ago, they put a congratulations message up on the marquee outside for two days, but then they took it down to make room to wish Mrs. G. a happy seventeenth anniversary as office manager.

"Well?" my mom said now. "What do you think?"

All I could think was that it was way cooler to announce a state beam champion than someone who'd just made the team, and how raised letters seemed pretty permanent, while the crappy plastic ones they put on the marquee at my old gym kept falling off so it read CONGRA S instead of CONGRATS. Rather than French-braiding each other's hair, we'd be competing for titles and medals, and it looked like the girls here were way ahead of me on that score.

Yeah, all of a sudden, the whole team thing didn't seem so exciting.

My mom was smiling at me again, and I forced myself to smile back. "It's awesome," I said. "When do I start?"

I started a couple of days later, once we'd had the chance to settle into our new house, which was one story high and smelled a little of stale smoke, although my mom said it was nothing a little Lysol wouldn't take care of. So now, it smells like stale smoke and Lysol.

"Oh, sugar," she said to me as we pulled up to the gym, this time in daylight. It wasn't said as an endearment, since my mom's not big on those. It was simply what she said when she wanted to say something else, but had to watch her language.

"What?" I asked.

"No, nothing," she said, giving me a hasty smile. "It's just that I forgot I was supposed to go in early this morning to meet the furniture delivery guys— we're getting a couple new rockers for the infant room. And there was a mom who wanted to talk to me about moving her son to the three-year-old group. I keep telling her we can't do that until he can use the big-boy potty, but you know how moms can be."

"Oh." I knew how *my* mom could be. She managed a day care center, and her job was the most important thing in the world to her. She had been wheeling and dealing on her cell phone the whole car ride down, and even though we've been in the South for less than seventy-two hours, she'd already spent a lot of them at the day care, making sure the transition was smooth.

"So . . . I take it you're not going to stay for the whole practice," I said.

She gave me another stressed-out smile. "Sorry, Britt. Maybe once I'm settled in at the day care, I can come watch you. You ready to go inside?"

"I guess," I said.

In the gym, everything was very white, and with

the harsh sunlight coming through the windows, it all looked bigger than it had in the shadows. The ceiling was high enough in this gym that there was no danger of the rhythmic girls throwing their hoops in the air and hitting it. That used to happen all the time at my old gym. The little kids couldn't throw their hoops hard enough for it to matter, but the competitive rhythmic girls would have to chase after the hoop when it bounced off the ceiling and went flying across the gym.

Rhythmic gymnasts used props like balls and ribbons and clubs as part of their routines, which consisted of more dancing and leaping and fewer tumbling skills. Of course, the brochure that I had found on my mom's nightstand said that this place didn't offer rhythmic classes. So all that extra ceiling height was a total waste.

The brochure also had biographies of the coaches, a couple who had emigrated from China, and featured a glossy picture of a very beautiful girl standing on one tanned leg, the other curved behind her until her toes almost brushed her dark ponytail. Was that the famous beam champion Noelle? Or was it just a model hired to look like a gymnast?

My mom headed straight for the front desk, which was over by the pro shop. At least this was familiar. Gyms *always* have pro shops, and they're inevitably right by the front desk, so that while parents are filling out boring paperwork, kids can roam around and decide which things they want to put on their gift wish lists. If I weren't so distracted right now, I could probably convince my mom to get me a three-pack of sparkly scrunchies.

There were three pillars dividing the front area from the gym, where I could see girls practicing on the beams (there were *twelve* beams—totally excessive!). I wanted to check the girls out, but my mom was beckoning to me.

"I'm Mrs. Morgan, and this is my daughter, Brittany," she said to the woman at the desk, placing her arm around me to draw me closer. "I believe we spoke on the phone? I faxed over the final enrollment paperwork yesterday."

The woman's name tag said MELANIE, and she was all business. "Level?" she asked, looking at me over the rims of her glasses.

She probably thought I was a Level Seven or something, since I'm so short. I'm twelve years old, but I look nine. You know you've got serious issues when you're a gymnast and you're *still* considered tiny. "I'm a Junior Elite," I said quickly.

"I see," she said. "Well, your group is just finishing up on the beam. You'll have to do some stretches first, of course, but would you like to join them now?"

I shrugged. "Sure, why not?"

"Mrs. Morgan, you're welcome to stay. We have a comfortable viewing area for the parents, and a full concession stand with snacks and drinks available."

I glanced at my mom, looking for some sign that she was at least *tempted*. That she was considering watching me practice, even for a second. It wasn't that she was a bad mother. She made sure I ate breakfast every morning, and on the weekends sometimes we would do something fun, like go to the aquarium or the mall. It's just, you know how little kids are always calling out to their moms when they're in the pool, or on top of the jungle gym? *Look at me! Mom, look!* I saw her glance at her watch, obviously worried about getting back to Ben and the big-boy potty, and wondered when she had stopped *looking*. She used to cheer when I did somersaults in the living room, but she hadn't even come to my last competition, because it was Parents' Night Out at the day care.

"Don't worry," I said to her before she could answer. "I'll be fine. And if I fall and break my neck, they have your info, right? So they'll call you."

"Britt, don't even joke about something like that," my mom said, giving a little laugh like, *Kids say the darnedest things, don't they?* "But I do have to get going. You behave yourself, okay? I'll be back to pick you up after practice."

"On time," I said. My mom had a habit of being late to *everything*. Her autobiography could have been titled *I'm on My Way: The Pamela Morgan Story*, because she's always saying she's "on the way" when in fact she's just about to jump into the shower, or she's still putting on her makeup.

"I'll do my best. But if I'm not here by then—" She dug through her purse, which was this huge lumpy designer thing that was like an abyss for receipts, credit cards, and cell phones. Finally, she pulled out a ten-dollar bill and handed it to me. "Just buy yourself a snack, all right?"

"Fine."

She tugged on my short blond ponytail and gave me a smile. She thinks it's the greatest thing that I'm a natural blonde, because she's not—she goes to the salon once a month to get her color touched up. She says by the time I'm her age, my hair will have turned a light brown, too, and that I'll be "pleased as punch" if and when I have a blond daughter who'll match my dye job and make it look natural. I'm not even kidding—she actually thinks about things like that.

Once she was gone, Melanie stood up to lead me toward the Excessive Beams. She nodded at my duffel bag, which had the name of my old gym, Loveland Gymnastics, emblazoned across the side. "Do you have a leo in there, or . . ."

I unzipped my hoodie, showing a shiny blue leotard underneath. "A girl's always gotta be pre-pared, right?"

She laughed. Now that my mom was gone, she didn't seem so uptight. "Very true. And your name is Brittany?"

"You can call me Britt," I said.

There were three girls practicing on the beams, and as we walked up, one of them did a perfect punch front tuck, landing squarely on the four-inch-wide balance beam. I do a back tuck in my routine, but it's not nearly as hard-core—you can see the beam as you come down, so it's easier to land. The punch front has a completely blind landing.

There was the Chinese woman I recognized from the brochure—the head coach, Mo Li—directing another girl, who was practicing full turns. "Keep your eyes focused ahead," Mo kept saying. "Look at one spot on wall. Are you looking at one spot?"

Full Turn Girl spun around once more and wobbled slightly. "I'm trying," she mumbled. I don't know if the coach heard her, but I did.

Maybe later, I thought, I could start up a conversation with Full Turn Girl. "Hey," I would say casually while we were at the fountain filling up our water bottles. "I totally feel you on the full-turn thing. I mean, 'do a complete three-sixty but keep your eyes on one spot?' How is that even possible?"

It was a start, but I'd have to make it funnier. "Did you ever see that movie where the girl gets possessed or whatever? My mom wouldn't let me watch it, but once I came downstairs to get a Coke and I saw the girl's head spinning all the way around. I bet you *she* could do that full turn, no problem!"

It would really have helped if I'd remembered the name of that movie, or if I'd seen more of it.

Maybe I'd just pretend I had seen the whole thing. Then Full Turn Girl wouldn't think I was a baby.

On the third beam, a tall girl with a long, curly ponytail executed a flawless full turn. I recognized her instantly: Brochure Girl. She was even more gorgeous than she'd looked in the picture, and I was suddenly very conscious of my small, pale legs and the way my too-short ponytail jutted out from my head instead of cascading down my back.

"Mo," Melanie said, trying to get the coach's attention, "this is Britt. She's the Junior Elite from Ohio."

Mo looked me over with sharp eyes, from my flip-flops with my bright pink toenails peeping out to the top of my white-blond head. "No gum," she said.

I'd played this scene in my head several times on the drive over and imagined many two-word introductions. *Hello, Britt,* maybe, or *Oh, fantastic!* or even *You're just the gymnast we've been waiting for!*—which is more than two words, but still. I hadn't really considered the idea that the first words my new coach would say to me might be *No gum.*

But I wanted to show her that I was serious, so I

swallowed it whole, making an exaggerated gulping sound, then smiled. "No gum," I agreed.

From her position high up on one of the beams, Brochure Girl rolled her eyes.

"I introduce you," Mo said. "Britt, these are your new teammates: Jessie, Noelle, and Christina."

Noelle was the one with the awesome punch front, so it made sense that she was the state beam champion. She had the perfect body for a gymnast, too—she was small and compact, like me, but *she* didn't look nine. Although she smiled at me when I looked at her, her brown eyes were very serious, and I knew she was going to be competition.

That's okay, though. I like a challenge.

Brochure Girl was Christina. She was slim, and supertall—for a gymnast, anyway. It'd be a while before I could even *dream* of being five feet tall, so anyone who came close seemed like a giant to me. She also didn't look very friendly. Maybe her pony-tail was too tight.

The girl who'd been struggling with the full turn was Jessie. She gave me a little wave, and I waved back. Suddenly the friendly conversation I'd imagined with her by the water fountain didn't seem so impossible.

I wriggled out of my pants, shoving them into my bag with my hoodie, and started to climb up onto one of the beams, but Mo shook her head. "We move to floor, but stretch first."

Mo quickly listed the succession of stretches she wanted us to do before walking over to talk to someone at the front desk. I didn't catch the exact order, but I figured I could just follow what everyone else was doing. Jessie took a spot on the floor next to me, and Noelle and Christina faced us, stretching out into a straddle position. This was my first chance to speak to them, and I tried to think of something to say. Something clever, preferably. Something that would make them think, Man, that new girl's all right.

"So," I said. "Is it all work and no play here, or what?"

Christina snorted. "It's an *Elite* gym," she said. "What did you expect? For us to take turns jumping on the trampoline?"

"No, that's not—" I tried to think of a better way to phrase it. "I mean, I was training Elite back in Ohio, too. I just meant . . ."

"Lay off, Christina," Jessie said, her voice muffled as she reached to touch her toes. She lifted her head, looking at me. "How long have you been in gymnastics?"

"I started when I was three," I said. "My mom says I was always doing somersaults and rolling off the couch, and she started to worry about me cracking my head open."

"That would explain a lot," Christina muttered.

I was kind of stunned by Christina's open animosity, and I couldn't formulate a decent comeback. I was grateful when Mo finally called us to line up at the corners of the forty square feet of blue carpet we called "the floor."

"Tumbling passes!" she said. "Warm up."

For several minutes, we took turns flipping across the floor. They weren't the passes we were actually going to do in competition or anything, just easy stuff, like handsprings and layouts, which are basically just flips with or without hands. No twists, no extra flips, nothing fancy. It got us ready for our big moves, and for me, it had the added benefit of getting me used to the floor.

Every floor mat is slightly different. This is weird, because they're regulation size and made out of the same materials, but each one has a different feeling under your feet. Like, the one at my old gym was a little spongier than this one, somehow. Even though I knew that the carpet was probably bought from the exact same place, the one at my old gym used to feel like you could sink your toes in it if you pressed down hard enough. This new floor felt nothing like that. It was like linoleum—flat and hard, but with springs underneath it, of course.

"Okay," Mo said, after telling me my legs had come apart as I did back handsprings. (This was not the first time I'd heard that, believe me. So far, the only solution I could think of was to superglue my ankles together. For this year's state competition, maybe I would try it.) "Jessie, you stay on floor to do combo pass. Other girls, to the pit."

The pit is the reason I am in love with gymnastics. Seriously, I want to marry it. The pit is where you get to do crazy tricks and land on an eight-inch-thick foam mat, and you don't have to worry as much about hurting yourself. If you're trying something really new, you get to do it and land in a pit filled with loose foam, which is like flipping into marshmallows, only less sticky. My old coach used to spot me on a triple tucked somersault in the loose foam pit, even though I probably never would've been able to do it on the actual floor. I hoped Mo was that cool.

I lined up behind Noelle and Jessie at the pit and glanced at Mo. "What should I do?" I asked.

"What *can* you do?"

I shrugged.

"Show me," Mo said.

Noelle did a back double pike into the pit, her body folded in half and rotating two complete times in the air. Then Christina turned out a double twist that was pretty good, I had to admit (when I did twists, I had a tendency to overdo them; at one competition back in Ohio, I just kept spinning like a cyclone, even when my feet had already hit the mat. I lost a few tenths of a point for stepping out of bounds on that one).

Then it came to me. All the other girls were lined up by the mirror on the wall, and they stared straight at me as I took a deep breath and prepared for my pass. I could feel Mo's eyes on me, too, and I knew this was big. I had to impress her. I had to impress *them*.

Technically, I hadn't done gymnastics in a week—I mean, other than some aerials in our brand-new front yard (which had a huge cactus in the middle of it—*not* good if your flipping gets a little wonky, like mine does sometimes), and I walked around the house on my hands until my mom told me to quit, but that was all. I knew I probably should play it safe on this first pass, and ease myself into it.

But that just wasn't my style. Instead, I ran as fast as I could, my arms pumping as my instincts took over, and then I was leaping into a round-off to a back handspring. I could feel the momentum in my body, and I knew I would pull it through before my feet even left the ground: a full-twisting double somersault.

I could've piked it to make it a little harder; it would've been the same move that Noelle had done, but with a twist added to make it interesting. But instead, I tucked my legs up close to my chest, just to be sure I could make it all the way around. I landed in the pit with room to spare, so I knew I would've rocked it if we'd been on the actual floor. As I sank into the soft foam, I threw my hands up in a salute, even though this wasn't a competition and there were no judges.

At least, not the kind who give you scores. I

heard light applause from Mo's direction. "Not bad," she said.

Just then, Christina burst into tears and ran for the locker room. Noelle shot me a look before heading after her.

I glanced at Jessie over on the floor.

"What?" I asked. "What'd I do?"

Jessie bit her lip, and her green eyes looked worried. "Christina's been trying to do that move for months," she said. "She can do it with a spot, but without one . . . she wipes out every time."

Later, I came up with about fifteen appropriate responses to that, like: *Oh, I'm sorry to hear that* and *Maybe I can help her*. But for some reason, my channel-surfing brain garbled the message, and I ended up blurting out a snarky line from one of the reality shows my mom liked to watch when she came home from work. "If you can't stand the heat," I said, "get out of the kitchen."

When the head chef on the reality show declared that exact same thing, all the contestants had laughed. But Jessie wasn't laughing, and I wondered how I was supposed to land on my feet when I always had one firmly planted in my mouth?

Two

Mo gave us a five-minute break, and Jessie joined the other girls in the locker room. Mo said it would be a good time for me to claim a locker and put my stuff away.

I really didn't want to go in there. I mean, I *wanted* to say something to Christina, but what? I barely understood what I'd done, much less how to fix it.

Then again, I felt kind of stupid hanging out all by myself. I inched over to the water fountain, but there was only so long I could pretend to gulp down the frigid water. I didn't *really* want to drink a lot, because then it would have sloshed around in my stomach for the rest of practice, and I hated that.

I thought about working on my leaps on the floor; my last coach had always been telling me I could use some serious improvement in that area. Don't get me wrong, I could jump super high, and getting at least a 180-degree split was absolutely no problem. But it was the whole too-much-energy thing again. Sometimes, I had trouble controlling my leaps and connecting them to other dance elements, which meant I lost valuable bonus points from my score.

But then I started imagining all the things they might be saying in there behind my back, and so I crossed over to the locker room and pushed the door open. Like the rest of the gym, it was state-of-the-art, with lockers that actually looked as if they'd been painted in this century. At Loveland, my old gym, I'd chipped almost all the orange paint off the front of my locker. If I'd stayed there for another month or two, I probably could've gotten the whole thing down to the metal.

"—big deal," Noelle was saying. "She's just a kid."

So, they *had* been talking about me. "Hey, guys," I said.

You know that phrase *If looks could kill*? Yeah, so did Christina, apparently. She was glaring at me with her dark eyes, her expression intensified by the sheen of tears.

Noelle and Jessie just looked uncomfortable. I decided to try to make amends. "Look, Christina, I'm sorry if—"

"How *old* are you, anyway?" Christina asked.

"I'm twelve," I said. At least that would make it better, right? That I wasn't some kind of wonder kid?

Although I did kind of like the idea of being a wonder kid.

"You're *twelve*?" Noelle said. "So am I. When will you be thirteen?"

"Next February." My birthday had just passed, so I hadn't been twelve for very long.

"I'll be thirteen in December," Noelle said.

"Cool," I said, turning to Christina and Jessie. "How old are you guys?"

"I'm fourteen," Jessie said, cautiously adding, "Christina is thirteen."

Christina just rolled her eyes.

I wondered if I should try to apologize again. "Hey," I said. "I'm really sorry that I upset you, with my full-in, I mean."

Sometimes gymnastics can be kind of confusing. If you do a double flip with a full twist on the first flip, you call it a full-in. If it's on the second flip, it's a full-out. And if you split the twist evenly between both flips, it's a half-in, half-out.

Maybe that explained why I was so good at math—even doing a floor routine could be like a word problem.

Christina stood up, and I remembered how much taller than me she was—I only came up to her chest.

Noelle picked at some dry skin on her hand (one of the many side effects of being a gymnast, unfortunately—all that chalk that we use makes our hands like parchment), acting as if she didn't even notice the tension between Christina and me. But Jessie's eyes darted between the two of us.

"Come on, Christina," Jessie said. "You know she didn't mean anything by it. So she can do a move that you can't; big deal. Maybe she could teach it to you, ever think of that? Then you could finally make the Elite team."

"Wait," I said. "You're not an Elite yet?"

Christina put her hands on her hips. "I practically am," she insisted. "I train with the Elite squad, don't I? I just haven't gotten the scores at a competition to make it official yet. So, please, spare me. Like I need *you* to teach me anything."

Um, excuse me. I wasn't the one who'd brought it up in the first place. It'd be like teaching a rattlesnake the etiquette of formal tea—totally impossible. Right then, I couldn't think of anything *less* appealing. Maybe beam reps. That was it.

"Hey," I said, holding up my hands defensively. "Don't take your failure out on me."

In my head, that hadn't sounded so harsh, but for a second, Christina looked seriously stung. I started to apologize for the second time. "Okay," I said. "It's like this. I—"

Just then, Mo came through the door. "Pity party over," she said, clapping her hands. "Yes?"

"Yes, ma'am," Christina said, her eyes lowered.

"Sometimes practice is hard," Mo said. "That makes you stronger. But we do not run out. This will not happen again."

"No, ma'am," Christina said, although it hadn't been a question, but more a command.

Mo looked at all of us. "Good," she said. "Now, back to work. Get your grips—we go to bars."

Once she'd left, I thought about trying one more time to fix things with Christina. But then she looked up, and I saw a new gleam in her eyes that made any words I'd been about to say stick in my throat. She'd been crying, but she wasn't hurt anymore. Now she was just mad.

I was beginning to somewhat get that T-shirt that said: DON'T MESS WITH TEXAS. 'Cause I had the feeling I had just messed with it, at least a little, and it didn't look pretty.

After bars practice with Cheng (Mo's husband and also the quietest man in the *universe*), we took a fifteen-minute snack break. I used my money to buy some apple slices and a Gatorade, and I was trying to find a place to eat by myself when Jessie gestured to me to come over.

"Hey," she said when I reached her table. "Come on, sit with me."

"Won't Christina and Noelle be mad?" I asked.

"Nah," she said. "They usually eat their snacks up front, by the pro shop. Christina's mom sometimes fills in at the front desk, since she practically lives here. Christina's dad is some big-shot cardiologist, so her mom doesn't need a job. Other than Christina and her gymnastics, at least."

I tried to remember who'd been sitting in the parents' viewing section. "Was she the woman with the long, wavy black hair?"

"Yup."

I noticed that Jessie didn't have anything in front of her, even though it was our snack break. I asked her if she needed to borrow some money, but she just shook her head.

"Oh, no," she said. "I'm not really hungry."

I was always starving after a workout, especially after doing something like floor, which required a lot of energy. But whatever. To each her own, I guess.

"So," I said, crunching on an apple slice. "Is Christina just mean, or does she not like me?"

Jessie hesitated.

"It's okay," I said. "You can tell me if it's me."

"Christina can be really sweet once you get to know her," Jessie said. "But I think she's just intimidated by you. I mean, you're only twelve, but you can do stuff that she can't *and* you're already Elite."

"Are you an Elite?"

Jessie made a face. "No," she said. "I have to compete at this Elite qualifier, too. Only Noelle is already Elite, but Christina and I are almost there."

When I became an Elite, I had been so excited. No more compulsory routines like in some of the lower levels, where you all have to do the exact same thing to the exact same mind-numbingly irritating music. And even after I'd gotten to do my own routines, the competitions were always held in some tiny gym with a handful of parents in the bleachers. But now, I'd hit the big time.

Elite is the absolute top level in gymnastics. Once you turn a certain age, you can become a Senior Elite instead of a Junior Elite, but that's it. Only Senior Elites can qualify for the Olympics, and there are tons of gymnasts who are awesome when they're juniors and then choke when they're seniors.

"Well," I said. "I hope you guys both make it. And I hope Christina gets over herself soon. I don't want to have to practice with her glaring at me."

"She'll come around," Jessie said. "We've been training together for three years, so it's just weird to have someone new in the mix. And Noelle's really nice—she's Christina's best friend, so she goes along with her a lot. Get her by herself and you'll probably end up being friends."

"Great," I said. "I'm glad that the girl who happens to *hate* me has so much influence. That's really encouraging."

Just then, Christina and her mom passed by, and I hurriedly popped an apple slice into my mouth, hoping it looked like I'd been chewing the whole time. I wondered if she'd heard me.

"You're not *trying* hard enough," Christina's mom was saying. She was just as beautiful as Christina, I noticed, with the same coloring and dark curly hair. "You have to put in a little effort."

"Mom, I'm working my butt off," Christina said. I raised my eyebrows and looked at Jessie.

"Obviously, it's not good enough," Christina's mom continued. "You think they give out medals for trying your best?"

"I know, I know."

"And now with that new girl, you're going to have to try harder."

Before I could look away, Christina glanced at me, and I knew from the look in her eyes that Jessie was wrong. She was *not* going to change her mind any time soon.

"She really doesn't like me," I said to Jessie.

"Well, I like you," Jessie said. "I'm glad you moved here. It was getting kind of old being third wheel to Christina and Noelle all the time."

I grinned at her. "Well, that's one thing you definitely don't have to worry about with me. Right now, you're the only wheel I've got."

For once, I was kind of grateful that the coaches had a strict no-talking rule during the final team conditioning and stretching exercises of the day. As much as it sucked having to sit in a split or straddle position until my legs were numb, it would've been way worse if I'd had to listen to the other girls whisper and snicker through the whole thing.

I was the first one packed up and out of there, even though I *knew* my mom still wouldn't be there to pick me up. I sat on the sidewalk in front of the entrance to the gym to wait for her. The early spring air was a little too cool to take my hoodie off, and my butt was like an icicle as the cold pavement cut through my thin workout pants. I tried to use the Jedi mind trick to make my mom hurry.

The door opened, and the other girls stepped out. They were giggling and talking, but they didn't see me. The way I knew this was that they kept laughing, instead of stopping to shoot me various dirty looks. I tried to seem nonchalant, so that if they did glance my way, they wouldn't think I'd been waiting for them. Because I hadn't.

"My mom said the sleepover is totally on," Christina was saying. It was weird to hear her talk in a normal tone that wasn't all snotty. "I got Rock Band, so I was thinking maybe we could make it a rock 'n' roll theme? What do you guys think? Oh, and of *course* we'll play Truth or Dare."

"Sounds like fun," Jessie said. "My stepdad won't let me go unless I clean my room, though. So I guess I'd better get on it."

"Clean *your* room? Don't you need to call in disaster relief for that?" Noelle said, and the girls giggled. See, if I'd said something like that, I would've gotten a huge eye-roll from Christina. Life is so unfair.

"Maybe cleaning Jessie's room should be a dare," Christina said. "It's the only way it'll get done."

"Hey," Jessie said. "I didn't ask *you* for a truth right now, okay? So leave me alone about my room."

"Whatever," Christina said. "This is going to be so fun! Way better than last year's, not that we didn't have an awesome time then, too. But we didn't even really *know* about Truth or Dare, and I didn't—"

Just then, Christina spotted me. I tried to paste on my nicest smile.

"*What*?" Christina demanded.

Supposedly, smiles are the universal language, but if that's true, Christina wasn't fluent. "Nothing," I said. "Your party sounds cool. I had a rock 'n' roll–themed party when I was ten, and we did karaoke. It was a blast."

"If you think it's so juvenile, I'd like to hear you come up with something better," she snapped.

"No, I—" Why did she seem to take everything as sarcasm? "I didn't mean it like that. I really do think it sounds cool."

"Well, I guess you'll never know," Christina said, "since I already sent the invites out before you got here. Sorry."

I knew that that had to be a lie. Who sent invitations to only two people? Like, what, Christina actually went out and bought one of those packets of ten or twenty invitations, took out two, and then handed them to Noelle and Jessie? Yeah, right.

"Christina—" Jessie began; I cut her off.

"That's a relief," I said, dragging my hand across

my forehead in an exaggerated *whew* gesture. "Saves me the awkwardness of having to turn you down."

Christina's mouth tightened.

"Sorry," Noelle said, shooting a glance at Christina. At least she looked a little apologetic. "We always have this big sleepover at Christina's over spring break. We've done it for the last couple of years—it's kind of a tradition. Maybe next year?"

Just then, the door opened again, and Christina's mom stepped out. Whereas my mom couldn't stay for five minutes to watch me land a move, Christina's mom had watched our entire practice from the bleachers. And from the way she chatted with parents bringing their toddlers in for tumbling class, and with the staff at the front desk, I could tell she was there a lot.

"Let's go, Christina," she said, putting her arm around Christina. "'Bye, girls!"

"'Bye, Mrs. Flores," Noelle and Jessie said in unison. But Mrs. Flores didn't reply—she was too busy leading Christina toward a shiny red SUV. Christina climbed in, but as the passenger-side door swung closed, I heard: "What was going on with your vaulting today? Hasn't Cheng told you—"

The door slammed shut.

"I'd better go, too," Noelle said. She was talking to Jessie, but she glanced at me at one point, as if she wasn't sure whether or not she should include me. Without her little boss Christina around, I guess she couldn't make decisions for herself. Well, I'd make it for her. I ignored her, pretending that the stripe down the side of my workout pants required my full and complete attention.

Noelle unchained a bike from a rack on the other side of the sidewalk, and I watched with some envy as she rode away. I wished I could just ride a bike home. Then I wouldn't have had to sit out here like a big dork waiting for my mom.

A car pulled up to the curb; Jessie started to open the passenger door before it stopped. "Um, do you need a ride?" she asked, leaning out.

"No," I said, a little more harsh than I'd meant to. I was really angry with my mother right now. Why did she always put me in this position?

Jessie just stared at me for a few moments, as if she was trying to figure me out. "Christina's not so bad," she said. "I know you didn't hit it off today, but don't worry about her."

"Thanks," I said. I decided to push my luck.

"Who knows, maybe she'll invite me to her sleepover."

Jessie smiled. "I don't know," she said. "Christina makes this sleepover into a really big deal. It's not like I haven't gone over to her house and played Rock Band before. But she plans this thing out like it's her wedding or something."

"If she wants help planning a *real* party, she should talk to me," I said. "My friend Dionne and I went paintballing once back home, and it was so much fun."

"That sounds fun," Jessie said. "Anyway, see you around."

Jessie got into her car, and as she rode away, I scanned the entrance to the parking lot for my mom's red Toyota. I knew I would probably be waiting for a while, but that was okay, now that I was alone again. And it gave me more time to daydream about how I was going to make the Texas Twisters see what I could bring to the table. I'd show Mo and Cheng my power and strength and flexibility, and I'd liven up practices and show the girls I could make them laugh. In a couple of weeks, they'd be thinking, How did we ever survive without Brittany Lee Morgan?

But as I sat there waiting, I thought of all the times I'd done this same thing back in Ohio. My mom would be running late, and I'd sit and wait at one of the picnic tables outside the gym. In April, Ohio was still chilly, and sometimes Dionne would wait with me, both of us shivering in our jackets more than was really necessary, in a silent contest to see who was colder. Occasionally, we would convince the concession stand at the aquatic center to spot us a hot chocolate, which we would split; then we'd beg our parents for the money to pay the concession back.

Now I felt the warmth of the sun on my face as I glanced left and right, taking in the low, flat buildings and the brown grass. My mother had said that I'd be feeling at home in no time, but right now I couldn't conceive of feeling that way about the Texas Twisters, much less this vast, lonely state.

Three

"**S**o, you liked your new gym?" my mom asked as she dished mixed vegetables out onto my plate. I hate mixed vegetables. Unless it's a packet of Skittles, there shouldn't be so many colors in one meal.

"It was okay," I said. We'd already been over this in the car, but it was like my mom was a reporter on one of those morning talk shows, and she only had so many index cards with questions on them. *How was school? How was gym? What are you watching?* Once she rattled through them, she just started back at the beginning.

Of course, my dad wasn't at dinner. This was

what happened when your mom ran a day care center and your dad was the head chef at a restaurant: your mom raised other people's kids, and your dad cooked other people's dinners. I knew lots of kids back in Ohio who'd probably have killed to have parents as completely uninvolved as mine. I mean, it *was* kind of a bonus that I got to do whatever I wanted, including have my run of the remote control when they weren't around. But sometimes it got lonely having a house all to yourself.

"Well, it's a *lot* more money than Loveland, that's for sure," my mom said. "So I hope it's better than okay."

The doorbell rang, and I sprang from my seat. "I've got it!" I yelled, even though there was no need. My mom had barely taken the napkin off her lap.

I knew who it was before I opened the door, but I still screamed when I saw her. "Grandma!"

"Miss Brittany Lee," she said, hugging me tightly to her. "How's my favorite little acrobat?"

"I'm fine. How's my favorite art historian?"

A corner of her mouth lifted. "I'm doing well, thank you. The weather is nicer here than in Ohio— but wait until the summer!"

I didn't really want to think that far ahead. It was still depressing me that I was here right now, so why get all sulky thinking about my long future in Austin?

"Do we have to start school again on Monday?" I asked. "Lots of the kids have spring break right now."

"Are the other girls in your gym on spring break?" my mom asked, coming out into the living room and butting in on our conversation. "Hello, Asta."

My parents were all about my grandmother living with us, but she said that she was just too "stuck in her ways." I don't know exactly what she meant by that, since, after all, she uprooted herself to move all the way out here. But she *is* stuck in her ways when it comes to that gross toothpaste that tastes like minted chalk, and the way she always reads the arts section of the paper first, followed by the editorials, and then finishes up with the crossword.

Both my mom and my grandmother were staring at me, and I remembered that I was supposed to be answering a question. "Oh, um," I said, "I don't know, actually."

Christina's sleepover was for the weekend

before spring break started, so I figured it must be coming up.

"Well, do they go to public or private, or are they homeschooled?"

"I . . . don't know."

My grandmother laughed. "And you're the one who wants to take a break from school? Seems like there's a lot you don't know."

As if there was a whole class I was missing out on, called Introduction to What Everyone Else in the Gym Is Up To. Without studying, I already had a pretty good idea—Christina was probably busy watching *Mean Girls* to figure out how to act, Noelle was following in her footsteps, and Jessie . . . well, at least Jessie seemed nice.

"Have you started reading *To Kill a Mockingbird* yet?"

The problem with being homeschooled by your grandmother was that she could hassle you about homework pretty much any time of any day.

"I can't find my copy," I said truthfully. "It might still be in a box somewhere."

My mom frowned at me. "You'd better find it," she said, "since I bought you that nice hardcover edition for your birthday."

The other problem with being homeschooled. I'd gotten some cool things for my birthday, including a metallic-looking leotard with straps that criss-crossed in the back, but I always received at least a couple of books for school. One Christmas, when my grandmother had wanted me to use a particularly expensive math workbook, it had been wrapped up and put under the tree. I'd almost rather have gotten socks.

From what I'd read on the back of the book, *To Kill a Mockingbird* seemed like a downer. It was all about the "pains of growing up," according to one reviewer. Why did I need to read about that? I was practically living it.

Later that night, after I heard the sounds of my mother and grandmother talking in the living room die down, I grabbed the portable phone from the hall and took it into my closet.

Even though every kid I know has a cell phone, my mom says children under the age of thirteen should not be dependent upon new technology. Whatever that means. But my friend Dionne has a cell phone, and I quickly dialed her number, hoping that she had her ringer turned down so her parents wouldn't go ballistic over the lateness of the call.

After a few rings, she finally answered.

"Hey," I whispered.

"Hey," Dionne whispered back. "How's the new life?"

"Sucky," I said. "How's the old one?"

"You know. Nothing's changed, it's all the same old thing."

We were quiet for a few moments. I don't know what Dionne was thinking about, but I was remembering the time that we tied fishing wire to one of the rhythmic girls' hoops, and, when she tried to reach for it, kept pulling it away from her. It was the funniest thing.

Now, my new gym doesn't even *have* rhythmic gymnasts, and I doubted the others would be able to appreciate a good prank like that.

"How's your new gym?" Dionne asked, as though reading my mind. Best friends are good at that.

"Tough," I said. "Everyone's so serious. And the girls are total snobs."

"Really?"

"Yeah," I said. "Like this girl Christina—she had

a complete meltdown because I could do a full-in and she couldn't. I'm surprised she didn't slap my face with a glove when we were in the locker room together."

There was some miniseries on TV all the time, starring a guy in a top hat and these really tight pants tucked into boots, who smacked another guy's face with a glove after an insult about a woman. I don't think I'm ready for a boy to feel that strongly about me, but when I am, I guess that'd be a nice way for him to show he cares.

"That's dumb," Dionne said. "Like it's your fault you're awesome."

"Plus, she's really good on the bars," I said. "And the beam. Like, *really* good. She looks like a professional ballerina or something, the way she points her toes and spins so perfectly."

"So maybe she's just full of herself."

"She's not getting any gold medal for congeniality, that's for sure," I said. "And then there's this other girl, Noelle. She seems all right, but she's, like, Christina's sidekick. As long as Christina decides to give me the stink-eye, Noelle will hate me, too."

"Is there anyone worth hanging out with?"

I thought about Jessie. Not only did she seem a little more laid back than the other girls, but she'd actually been nice to me today. But for some reason, I didn't want to mention her—just in case she turned out to be a snob-in-nice-girl's clothing. I'd have hated to look pathetic, talking her up now only to find out she was just like the rest of them. "Maybe," I said. "We'll see."

"You're probably getting up insanely early to train, huh?"

"Yeah," I said.

At Loveland, I didn't start training until eight o'clock, since I was homeschooled and also the only Elite girl there. So I'd gotten a lot more one-on-one time with the coach, while all the other gymnasts were at school. At Texas Twisters, training started at six thirty sharp, and all the Elite girls were expected to be there. They also didn't do a whole lot of private sessions with only one gymnast, because apparently they thought that "an atmosphere of cooperation and competitiveness pushes gymnasts to be their very best." Believe me, if they had done one-on-ones, I'd be all over it by now.

"Hey," Dionne said. "I have an idea that will help you make friends there. Try a prank."

I rolled my eyes, even though Dionne couldn't see me. "It's not really that kind of gym, Dee."

"Only because they haven't experienced the true genius of one of Brittany Morgan's practical jokes. Remember that time you switched the sugar with the salt, and Coach had to gulp down that whole Gatorade just to wash out the taste of salty coffee?"

I smiled at the memory. It had been truly classic, but I still couldn't see Mo or Cheng having a good laugh about a joke at their own expense. They'd probably just make me do a hundred push-ups and run around the gym a billion times.

"Just think about it," Dionne said. "It could break the ice."

"Okay," I promised. "If a good opportunity presents itself, I'll consider it."

"Well, I have to get going—as cool as my mom is, she'd ground me from my cell phone if she caught me talking on it after ten at night."

"It's only nine fifteen," I said, glancing at my alarm clock.

"Man, it's true what they say about home-schooled kids, huh?" Dionne said. "You go on field trips to museums and spend hours talking about philosophy, but when it comes to time zones, you're clueless. You know how TV shows always say 'eight, seven central'? You're in central now."

Of course. How perfect that Dionne had already moved on, while I was stuck in the past.

Four

If I had to rank the four gymnastics events in order of real-world practicality, it would have to go like this: floor, vault, bars, beam. Floor makes the most sense, considering it's basically another version of what humans walk on all the time. Sure, ours has springs under it and a white line all around that you're not supposed to step past, but otherwise it's the same. We just do more flips on ours.

Vault is pretty logical, too. What if you had to jump over a fence? Not because you were a criminal or anything, but maybe because you were running from a criminal. Or a mean dog. Vaulting teaches me to run superfast and jump over something, but also how to twist and turn in the air so I look cool while I do it. That's clearly helpful.

Bars are more of a stretch, but I can still see *some* sort of point to them. If I ever had to hang from a tree limb for a really long time—like if I was climbing out of a burning building or something—I could totally do it. My hands are all calloused and ripped up from swinging on the bars, so the rough bark probably wouldn't even hurt that much. And with my upper body strength, I could pull myself up on the branch to wait out the fire if I needed to. Although I hope the tree's not *too* close to the burning house in this scenario, considering that wood is highly flammable and all.

But beam? I just don't get it. It's like: here, balance on this four-inch-wide surface, and while you're at it, throw out crazy tricks that are bound to make you wobble or fall. And then, of course, you'll lose massive points from your score if you *do* fall, even though only a moron would've tried to do a full twist on that narrow a surface anyway.

So, of course I was thrilled to find out that beam was our first morning event after warm-ups.

"This is cruel and unusual punishment," I

muttered as I rummaged through my gym bag for my beam shoes. I tried to say it low enough that Mo wouldn't hear me and so that it would seem as if I was just talking to myself, but at the same time loud enough that one of the girls would hear.

Okay, if I were being honest, I kind of hoped they would hear. After all, if there's one thing any gymnast can bond over, it's how much morning practice really sucks. Especially on beam.

But if Jessie and Noelle heard me, they didn't acknowledge it. Instead, they climbed up on two of the beams and started their tiptoe walks from one end to the other. It's an exercise that's supposed to help with balance, but it also bears a striking resemblance to torture.

Christina heard me, though. Just my luck. "If you don't like it," she said, "don't do it."

She climbed onto a beam, leaving me alone on the floor, clutching my beam shoes. A lot of the girls at my old gym had used them, but now I saw that I was the only one here who did—the three other girls were barefoot. I wondered if they thought beam shoes were babyish.

Whatever. If any of them tried to say something about my shoes, I decided I would just point out the stuffed Dalmatian I had seen poking out of Noelle's bag. I mean, if *that* was okay, then beam shoes, by comparison, were the height of sophistication.

I glanced around the gym, but Mo was over by the front desk, talking to someone who was hidden by one of the pillars. *Try a prank.* That's what Dionne had told me. *It'll break the ice.*

Before thinking it through, I swiped Noelle's stuffed dog and shoved it into my bag. Later, when the girls weren't watching, I'd find something really hilarious to do with it, like putting it in the middle of the vaulting table or setting it up to look like it was manning the front desk. It'd be classic.

"What's so funny?" Jessie whispered to me once I'd climbed up on the beam next to her. But Mo was coming, and anyway, I really wanted to see the look of surprise at my comic genius on everyone's face. So I just shook my head, stretching my arms straight out from my body as I began my tiptoe walk down the length of the beam.

The other girls stopped and turned to look at something, but I just concentrated on keeping my balance, feeling every muscle in my calves pulling as I reached the other end of the beam.

"Uh-oh," Christina said out of the corner of her mouth. "Noelle's future husband is here."

Noelle hushed her, although I did notice that Noelle's face turned abnormally red, and it couldn't have been from exertion, because, in spite of the fact that I personally hated these pointless beam exercises, they were far from being the most strenuous things we did.

"Don't try to hide it," Jessie teased. "There's nothing to be ashamed of. He's cute!"

Mo arrived just in time to catch us talking and gave us a sharp look. One thing I'd learned in the few practices I'd had so far: Mo and Cheng took gymnastics very seriously. Our leotards might as well have been those orange vests people wore when they picked up trash on the side of the road— the second we put them on, it was time to work. I missed the atmosphere back at Loveland, where Dionne and I had been able to scheme and giggle all through practice.

I executed my half turn at the end of the beam, sneaking a peek to see this guy the girls were talking about. Personally, I didn't see anything special about him. He was wearing a faded gray shirt with BIRCHBARK HIGH SCHOOL emblazoned across the front of it, and a pair of those baggy shorts that basketball players wear. His dark hair was way too curly (in my opinion), and he had a little bump on his nose. But the way the girls were drooling over him, you'd think that he'd stepped right off the cover of a teen magazine and started doing chin-ups on the high bar.

Of course, I wasn't about to mention that I thought he looked like a dork. Not when I was only a prank away from getting them all to see that practice could be fun—that *I* could be fun.

Because Mo was watching, Noelle tried to look as if she was working on her dance series instead of sneaking peeks at the boy. But it was so obvious it was kind of funny.

"Posture, Noelle," Mo said. She must've noticed Noelle's distraction, too, because there didn't appear to be anything wrong with her posture—other than the fact that she was craning her neck to scope out the cute guy.

"Jessie, I need to see at least one hundred eighty degrees on leaps," Mo added.

This woman did not play around.

The cute guy was now doing handstand push-ups on the parallel bars. Apparently, he didn't play around, either. Although I didn't really see his appeal, I did have to admit that that was pretty impressive to watch. I could probably have done five of those before getting tired or bored, but he was still going.

"You have all seen Scott train before," Mo said, exasperated; I whipped my head around so she wouldn't think I was one of his admirers. "He is training for the college team this fall. In some years, maybe you will get scholarship like him. But it won't happen if you don't *practice.* So I want to see your series—Christina, go."

As though Mo had whistled loudly or clapped her hands, Christina took her position at the end of the beam, looking taller than ever as she stretched both arms above her head. One minute she was facing backward, clenching the fingers of one hand with the other, and then all of a sudden she was flipping. She did a flawless Onodi to twist herself into a forward-facing position, and then executed two elegant front aerial flips in a row.

Front flips with no hands are *tough.*

"Good," Mo said. "But do not pause so much after first element. Square your body, and go right into second. They should flow, yes?"

As far as I was concerned, Christina had been flowing so much she was practically Niagara Falls. But what did I know?

"Jessie, go," Mo said, and Jessie launched into two back handsprings and a layout that got high above the beam, finally landing on both feet. Which, on a four-inch beam, is not exactly a cakewalk. Most moves on the beam have you landing one foot in front of the other, to make it easier.

Mo grunted. "Britt, go."

I'd been working on a tucked full twist back at my old gym, but didn't quite have it down yet. Still, I figured, why not give it a whirl? I took a deep breath and did my round-off, but as soon as my feet hit the beam, I knew my center was off. I could feel my body leaning one way, trying to twist before I actually got into the air. Rather than crash and burn, I balked, stopping in the middle of the move and jumping off the beam.

Mo just nodded. "Your series will be round-off to layout with two-foot landing," she said. "You need to refine before you add twist."

Okay, so obviously I was still struggling with my full twist. But how was I supposed to learn it if I didn't even get to practice it?

I barely heard Mo signal Noelle to go, but all of a sudden, she was flipping across the beam. And then her foot must've slipped or something, because her third layout lacked a lot of height. She missed her landing on the beam and ended up with both feet on the mat, a startled expression on her face.

"Again," Mo said. I saw Noelle glance at Scott over on the parallel bars, but I doubted he was even paying attention to her. Why would a high school guy care about a twelve-year-old gymnast practicing her beam routine?

We were all supposed to continue working on our dance series, but none of us could take our eyes off Noelle as she climbed back onto the beam. I'm sure Christina and Jessie were thinking exactly what I was: Come on, come on. You can do this.

Noelle took a long time setting up for her pass, making sure that her feet were in a straight line on the beam and her arms up by her ears. Finally, she launched into the series—one, two, three, and then, *bam*! She split the beam on her way down and found herself belly-flopping onto the mat, her face hitting the blue vinyl with a sickening smack.

Even though I barely knew Noelle, and still had no clue how she felt about me, I almost jumped down to make sure that she was okay. But neither Christina nor Jessie made a move, so I just stood there, unsure of what to do. Was there some rule about comforting fallen gymnasts? Was it like a war zone? Each girl for herself, with no time to go back for anyone left behind?

Noelle barely flinched, though. Her expression was stoical as she got to her feet, placing her hands on the beam like she was going to go again.

Mo stopped her. "Okay," she said. "Get a drink of water. Girls, I need to see your dance series. Let's go!"

Considering we all had our own water bottles, I figured that sending Noelle to the water fountain was just a way to make her take a break for a second. This time, when she walked by the area where Scott was training, she kept her eyes straight ahead.

"We need to choreograph new beam routine," Mo said, watching me as I did a series of mincing dance steps and struck a small pose. "This one is choppy."

It's not that I disagreed with her. My beam routine involved a lot of quick, jarring motions with my hands, where I whipped them up above my head and then back down again. It made me look like a toy that had been wound up too tightly.

But still. This was the routine that my old coach had worked with me on, the routine that had gotten me Elite status. This was the routine that was *supposed* to include a tucked full twist, instead of some lame back layout.

"Where's Sparky?" Noelle asked, holding her open gym bag, which held a neatly folded workout suit and extra leotard, but no stuffed Dalmation.

Mo was watching Jessie do a scale and barely glanced up. "Hmm?" she said.

"Where's my stuffed dog? Where's Sparky?" Noelle demanded, and now her voice sounded really strained, as if she'd been crying or was about to be.

Oh, crap. My eyes immediately went to my gym bag, which was zipped up, thank goodness. I could make out the vague outline of a stuffed animal in there, but surely it was just because I knew what to look for. Right? No one else would be able to tell that the dog was in there.

"Someone took Sparky," Noelle said, and now she was definitely crying. Her face was splotchy and red, and she was frenziedly emptying her gym bag. "No wonder I can't stay on the beam. Sparky hasn't left my gym bag for three years. Who would take a stuffed animal?"

Mo was paying attention now. Everyone was, including Scott, who'd stopped doing press hand-stands and was looking in our direction.

What had I done? Noelle wasn't supposed to know that her dog was gone until I'd had the chance to think of something funny to do with it. By then, everyone would have been laughing, and there'd have been no way she could get mad.

But nobody was laughing, least of all Noelle. Just my luck: the first prank I tried to pull involved Noelle's special charm. But how was I supposed to have known that?

"Are you sure you had Sparky today?" Mo asked calmly.

"I told you, that dog *never* leaves my gym bag. Aren't you listening?"

Christina and Jessie exchanged a shocked look. I hadn't heard Noelle snap at anyone like that before, much less the coach.

"Maybe we should look in the locker room," I said. If only I'd had a second alone I could have taken the stuffed animal out of my bag and put him somewhere else, like in one of the younger gymnasts' cubbies or something. Noelle might have thought it a little weird, but at least she wouldn't have thought I'd purposely stolen her good-luck charm.

Just then, Scott walked over. Up close, I guess he looked a little cuter than I'd previously thought. He had really blue eyes, for one thing. But I still didn't see anything to swoon over.

"What's up?" he asked. "Is there anything I can do to help?"

Noelle just put her head in her hands, emitting a weird muffled noise when Christina patted her on the back.

Mo shook her head. "Cheng will be here soon to work with you on tumbling," she said to Scott. "We need to get back to practice, too."

"I can't practice without Sparky!" Noelle wailed, lifting her head. "You saw what happened. I almost killed myself!"

"Where did you last see Sparky?" Scott asked. I had to give him credit. He somehow made it sound like a legitimate question, instead of letting it seem as if he was asking, *What's your problem, psycho?* Which is the way it would've sounded coming out of my mouth.

"Right here, this morning," Noelle said. "He was in my gym bag when I got ready. Then I went to grab my water bottle to fill it up, and he was gone."

Her voice broke on the last word, and I considered coming clean. I could just say it was an accident. But what, like someone else's stuffed animal just *fell* into my gym bag? Everyone would think I was a thief.

I considered explaining the prank idea, but when I actually imagined saying it out loud, it sounded really dumb. And also like a flimsy excuse that I'd made up on the spot, to hide the fact that I was a thief.

The only way to do it would be to find a way to distract everyone again, and then make the switch when no one was looking. Maybe I could think of another prank to redirect their attention. If only I'd known how to throw my voice.

"Well, why don't we start here?" Scott said. "Everyone, empty your gym bags, and if he's not in any of them, we can check the lost-and-found."

I take it back—Scott was *not* cute. He was obnoxious. "I think I see Cheng waiting for you," I said.

"Britt," Mo said warningly, but Scott just smiled.

"I know what it's like to depend on a good-luck charm," he said, winking at Noelle. "On the morning of big meets, I always put on the same pair of socks. They're full of holes, now, but I won't trade them for anything."

That sounded kind of gross.

Jessie and Christina were already down from their beams and had unzipped their bags and turned them inside out. I started to seriously sweat. Would the gym kick me out for stealing?

"Why don't you look in your bag?" Mo said, cocking her head toward me.

"But why would it be in there?" I asked. I could feel this terrible itch on the bridge of my nose, but I'd watched a whole TV program about how little tics like scratching a nose or pulling at an ear were dead giveaways of liars. "It's probably sitting on her dresser at home or something, and we're just wasting time."

"Perhaps so," she said. "But Noelle will not feel comfortable unless we look."

"Fair enough," I said. I tried to make it sound breezy, but I think it came off as more wheezy instead. "I'll check out the locker room. That would make the most sense."

Mo's gaze grew sharp. "Why don't you just open your bag?" she said. "Noelle will feel better once every possibility has been eliminated."

I could feel my face turning red as I leaned down to unzip my gym bag, immediately revealing a patch of black-and-white spotted fur inside.

Noelle gasped. "Sparky!" She reached into my bag and snatched the dog, clutching it to her chest as if it was her most prized possession. If you asked me, she was just hamming it up.

"I was going to give it back," I said, but it sounded weak even to my ears. Why did I have to make the truth sound like a lie? I *had* planned to return the dumb dog. "It was just going to be a little joke. I was going to do something funny, like put it on the vaulting table or . . . whatever."

Mo looked at me with an expression that made my throat tighten. It wasn't even like she was angry. It was more like she'd just found out that I was a completely different person from who she thought I was. "We don't touch other people's personal property," she said. "Ever. Not even for joke. Understand?"

"Yes," I said, raising my chin. Noelle was staring at me as if I was the devil, Christina looked ready to punch me, and Jessie was shaking her head. At least stupid Scott and his stupid nose that he liked to stick into other people's business had walked away. As if I needed one more member of this jury, which had all decided I was totally guilty.

I would *not* cry.

"Are we ready to go on?" Mo asked, her tone letting us know that there was only one answer. "We've lost enough time."

"Yes," the other girls answered in unison.

Mo looked at me.

"I'm ready," I whispered.

As I passed by Noelle to climb up on my beam, I wanted to tell her I was sorry. But she wouldn't meet my gaze, and I didn't know how to say it. So instead I just went back to working on my choppy hand movements.

It was a badly choreographed routine, but at least I'd done it a million times before. So when my eyes got too watery to see the beam, it didn't really matter.

Five

A t Texas Twisters, it was a tradition every Friday after practice for the Elite girls to go get frozen yogurt. It was supposed to build team spirit or something.

Technically, if you really wanted to get down to it, we were not all Elite. Noelle and I both were, but neither Jessie nor Christina had qualified yet. In fact, that was why Christina was so determined to get that tucked full-in on floor—Mo told her she had to upgrade her level of difficulty if she expected to make the Elite team.

Ever since the incident with Sparky, Christina had been shooting me death glares in practice, Noelle had been ignoring me, and Jessie just lifted her shoulders in a helpless gesture, like, *It'll get better.*

How can you have team spirit when you're part of a team that doesn't completely exist, and where nobody trusts you?

Jessie and Noelle rode with Christina and her mom, since she came to every practice. They didn't invite me to join them, but whatever. Mrs. Flores must have driven one of those newfangled SUVs with only four seat belts. Right.

Mo drove me to the yogurt place. Cheng was back at the gym, since, as Jessie said, "If it doesn't directly deal with gymnastics, he's like a fish out of water." Apparently, once he'd had to attend a banquet, when Noelle made the Elite team, and he had just sat there shredding his napkin until Mo told him to go on home.

At first, it was superquiet—Mo didn't even play music in the car, which struck me as the weirdest thing ever. She didn't seem to be in the mood for conversation, either, but I decided to start one up anyway.

"So," I said, "I can totally do a full twist on beam, you know. I just messed it up before. But you should really think about putting it back in my routine, because that's the move that's going to get me to the Olympics someday."

Okay, so the last part might have been an exaggeration, but that move would definitely have gotten me there faster than a stupid layout, that's for sure.

"You want to go to the Olympics?" Mo asked.

Duh. Doesn't everyone? Mo's voice hadn't lost its calm, even tone, so I wasn't sure how she meant the question. Was she surprised because she didn't think I could make it? Was she just curious? Was she bitterly reflecting on her own missed opportunity? I'd read in my mom's brochure that Mo had been all set to make the Chinese Olympic team when she was eighteen, but that they'd replaced her with a vault specialist at the last minute, and that by the time the next Olympics rolled around, she had been past her prime.

"Um, yeah," I said.

"Toe point get you to Olympics," Mo said. "Clean lines. Consistency. Hard work. Those get you to Olympics."

"Right," I said. "I know. All of those things, and awesome moves, like a full twist on beam. It qualified me as Elite, didn't it?"

"I saw that competition," Mo said. "Full twist was good, but not good enough. You not ready."

"What do you mean, you saw that competition?"

This time when she glanced at me, there was a slight sparkle in her eyes. "You think I sign just anyone for my gym?"

This was the first I'd heard about there having been any sort of audition. Had she seen me compete and approached my parents? Or had they sent her a tape, and had she then invited me to come? I had so many questions, but when I opened my mouth to speak, Mo just shook her head.

"You know what else get you to Olympics?" she said. "No talking. Just doing."

That seemed to be the Li family motto, because Cheng hadn't spoken more than ten sentences to me during the last week I'd been training. And Mo didn't say another word until we reached the yogurt place.

To be honest, I'm more of a straight-up ice-cream girl. But welcome to the world of Elite gymnastics, I guess—from here on out, it was all about the frozen yogurt.

Jessie's mom was waiting for us, having headed over directly from her job. She'd brought a couple of bags of chips—"After a long day at work, I need something more substantial than yogurt," she said—and she offered Jessie the sour-cream-and-onion ones, but Jessie refused.

"I thought they were your favorite," Jessie's mom said.

"They *were*," Jessie mumbled. "They're just not anymore."

It was the first time I'd met Jessie's mom, so I introduced myself, and when she offered me the bag of chips, I wasn't about to turn them down. Jessie might not have wanted that sour-cream-and-onion goodness, but I loved it. I'd go straight for the ones at the bottom, that had the most seasoning on them, and then I'd lick it off my fingers. Yum.

Jessie got a cup of 99 percent fat-free white chocolate mousse; Christina got a parfait; and Noelle ordered mango sorbet. Finally, it was my turn, and I chose root beer–flavored yogurt. At least it would be interesting.

Mrs. Flores also ordered mango sorbet, winking at Noelle. "If you're going to be good, then I will, too," she said. "Christina, I can get you an extra cup and you can split my sorbet, if you want."

"No, Mom," Christina said, rolling her eyes. It was good to know I wasn't the only one who inspired that response. "I always get the parfait."

"I know that," Mrs. Flores said. "But yogurt still has milk in it. Sorbet is just fruit."

"It still has, like, a million pounds of sugar," Christina said, but she gave in, canceling her order and asking the attendant for another Styrofoam cup for her half of the sorbet.

I wouldn't have changed my order, but I still didn't get why Christina seemed to be so dismissive of her mom. Mrs. Flores actually cared about the skills Christina was learning and how she was doing in practice. And she dressed like a magazine model, with fancy alligator shoes and really heavy eyeliner.

When our orders were up, Mo and the two moms took theirs to one table, and Jessie, Noelle, and Christina sat at another. For a minute I almost considered sitting with the adults, but that was just too lame. So instead, I took a deep breath and joined my teammates.

"Hey," I said brightly, pretending I didn't see them glaring at me. "Gotta love frozen yogurt, huh?"

The girls just licked their spoons, like I wasn't even talking.

"I think frozen yogurt can tell you a lot about a person," I said. "It's like a Magic 8 Ball. Want to know what your choices say?"

"What does root beer–flavored yogurt mean?" Christina sneered. "You're immature?"

I blinked at her. "How is root beer immature?" I asked. "I've seen adults drink it. My dad loves root beer. And it has the word *beer* in it, which is definitely grown-up, since kids aren't allowed to have beer."

Christina went back to licking mango sorbet from her spoon, but this time I could tell it was because she couldn't think of anything to say. Point for me.

"Anyway," I said, "if you want to know what *my* choice means, it's that I'm fun. I don't pick something superboring, like sorbet. I'm not afraid to try something new."

"Like a full twist on beam?" Christina snickered.

"Like a full-in on floor," I countered.

Point two for me.

"What does mango sorbet say?" Noelle asked finally. It seemed as if she'd calmed down since the Sparky incident. She wouldn't look me in the eye, but because she was now sitting next to me, she didn't really have to. So it was easier to pretend that she wasn't still mad at me.

"Hmm." I let a spoonful of root beer yogurt

melt on my tongue while I thought about it. "Mango sorbet says that you're refreshing. You're simple, but not in a bad way. It's more like you don't believe in hiding behind a lot of crap. And the color of mango sorbet is bright and cheerful, so you're an optimist."

"I don't know about that last part," Noelle said, letting out a little laugh.

"But I got sorbet, too," Christina said. "How can it mean the same thing for both of us?"

"It doesn't," I said, trying not to sound as if I were just talking off the top of my head. Which, of course, I totally was. "Noelle got sorbet because she wanted it, so it reflects her true personality. Your mom thought it was healthier, so all that shows me is that she cares about her appearance. And you got it because your mom made you, so that makes you kind of a pushover."

"You know," Christina said, dropping her spoon into her cup of sorbet so hard that drops of orange splattered on the table. "I used to look forward to this."

I don't know how I manage to mess *everything* up, but somehow I do. "Sorry," I said. "I was trying to make conversation, that's all. No big deal. Let's just eat our yogurt."

For a moment it seemed as if I'd accidentally said, "Let's whittle the tips of our plastic spoons into points and stab each other in the eye," because that's totally what Christina looked like she was going to do. But she just sighed.

"Whatever," she said.

For the next few minutes, we lived up to the Li family motto that silence is golden. The only sound was that of Jessie, slurping slightly on her spoonful of yogurt. I think it was the same one she'd started with, and she still hadn't eaten it all.

"Noelle," I said, because I can always be counted on to break up an awkward moment. Or to create one. "Is there any story to your name? I was just wondering, because I think it's really cool."

"Oh," Noelle said. It was obvious that she was struggling with her natural politeness and her simultaneous desire never to talk to me again; the politeness won out. "Um, actually, my first name is Nicoleta. My parents made my middle name Noelle, because I was born on Christmas. So that's just what I go by."

"Nicoleta?" I repeated. "Wow, that's even cooler. What is that, French or something?"

"Romanian," Noelle said, and for the first time

she met my gaze. "My mom was an Elite gymnast back in Romania. My parents defected to the States just a year before I was born."

"No wonder you're so awesome at gymnastics," I said. Now that she mentioned it, she looked Romanian, too. I'd seen some footage of Nadia Comaneci on the internet, and that was what Noelle looked like—straight brown hair pulled back in a ponytail, serious brown eyes. "What's your last name?"

"Onesti."

I had to ask her to spell it, which was good, because it was completely different from what I would've guessed. Based on the pronunciation, I probably would've spelled it Ohnesht.

After that, I asked both Jessie and Christina for their full names. I think names also tell you a lot about a person, possibly more than dessert choices do. Jessie mentioned that her name was Jessica Marie Ivy, which fit her. Her eyes were the color of ivy, so the last name would be easy to remember.

I could tell Christina didn't want to answer, but that she knew it would seem too rude not to, after the other girls had. So she told me her name was Aurelia Christina Flores. How's that for a crazy cool name?

"How come you two go by your middle names?" I asked.

Noelle shrugged. "My parents just started calling me Noelle," she said, "and I guess it stuck."

"It's very common in Mexican culture to go by your middle name," Christina said, almost belligerently, as if I was stupid for not knowing that. "Aurelia's my grandmother's name, but I'm called Christina so we don't get confused."

"Neat," I said.

Nobody asked me about my name, but I didn't care. At least they were talking to me a little bit.

"So . . . are you still having that sleepover?"

Christina made a face, twisting a long strand of her black hair around her finger. "No, it's totally off."

"Wow, that was quick," I said. "Well, maybe we can have one at my house instead. When is your spring break again?"

I knew Christina elbowed Jessie in the ribs, because I saw Jessie wince. "Of course it's not *off*," Christina said. "I was being sarcastic. It's next weekend, and it's going to be an absolute *blast*. Sorry—it was kind of planned before you came here."

"Otherwise I'd be invited for sure," I said, finishing her sentence for her. "Right, I got it. It can be hard to work in—what, *one* more person?—on such short notice."

"Well, it's kind of a Texas Twisters party," Christina said. "You know, our last really big thing before the competition season starts and we have to get more serious."

It was hard to imagine them becoming *more* serious. Although my mom had put me in some tumbling classes at the local YMCA, I hadn't really considered doing gymnastics as a sport until a friend of mine had her fifth birthday party at a gym. We got to play around on the equipment, just walking the length of the beam or swinging from the lower bar, and ever since then, that's what gymnastics was for me. Playing. Having fun.

"I'm a Texas Twister now," I said, even though I'd meant to drop it, not wanting Christina to think I was begging to go to her stupid party.

"Yeah," Christina said, wrinkling her nose. "But, you know. Not really."

"I'm an Elite, aren't I?" I shot back. "Whereas *you—*"

"Hey," Noelle cut in, glancing anxiously back and forth between Christina and me, "you never told Jessie what her yogurt flavor says about her."

"Oh," I said. "Well . . . she picked white chocolate mousse, so that tells me that she's very decadent."

"Decadent?" Jessie asked, pausing in midbite.

My grandma uses that word all the time when she takes me to museums, to describe baroque artwork, so I forget that not everyone my age knows it. "Yeah, decadent. You enjoy nice things. You don't have a problem treating yourself to something really rich and, um . . . decadent."

Jessie slowly lowered her spoon back to her cup. All of a sudden, her face looked as white as her yogurt. "Excuse me," she said, and then she pushed her chair back and headed for the restroom. Jessie's mom reached out to stop her, then shrugged at Mo as Jessie brushed past.

I just stared at the spoon, which had a small pat of yogurt in it that was now turning into a puddle. "That was weird."

"Not really," Christina said. "So far, you've made Noelle and me cry, so why not Jessie, too?"

That stung. I hadn't *meant* to make anyone cry; why did I seem to upset every single person I spoke to? Especially Jessie, who was the only one who'd been semi-nice to me. "I don't get it," I said. "What'd I say?"

Christina shrugged. "With Jessie, who knows? She can be sensitive sometimes."

You mean, a girl who sobs because of a stupid gymnastics move, or a girl who makes a fool out of herself because of a stuffed animal? I wanted to say that, but I didn't. Instead I just got up, tossing my empty cup into a nearby trash can. "Well, I'm going to go see what's up," I said.

I knocked on the outer bathroom door, even though I knew it was the kind that had a bunch of stalls and I could have just walked right in. I didn't want Jessie to feel as if I was crowding her.

"Jess?" I said, stepping inside. Okay, so she'd never told me I could shorten her name even more than it already was, but that's just how I rolled. I made someone cry for completely random reasons, and then I overstepped the bounds by using a nickname. I liked to think it was part of my charm.

"Jess?" I said again, leaning down to look under the stall doors. In the handicapped stall, I saw the yellow flip-flops that Jessie'd been wearing, but they weren't flat on the floor. Instead, it looked as if she was on her knees. "Jess? You okay?"

There was a quick flush, and then the stall door opened. Just to be sure I hadn't imagined it, I glanced at her knees. They were red and had lines imprinted on them from the tiles.

"Everything all right?" I asked. "Sorry if I made you upset. I don't know what I am saying half the time."

She crossed over to the sink and splashed cold water on her face. When she lifted her head, our eyes met in the mirror. "It's cool," she said. "Don't worry about it. It was nothing you said."

"Are you sure?" I asked. "Because all of a sudden you just got up and left . . ."

"I'm fine," she said, smiling. Her face was ruddy, and it almost looked as if she'd been sweating. But of course, she'd just splashed water on her face. So that must have been it. "I just didn't feel well. It was probably the yogurt—I usually don't eat that much."

"You barely ate any."

"Because I wasn't feeling well," Jessie said slowly, as if she was talking to an idiot. "Come on. Let's get back out there."

"Okay," I said. "If you're sure that we're cool. Honestly, you're the only one who's actually been nice to me, so I'd hate to think I'd screwed that up somehow."

"You haven't," Jessie said, putting her arm

around me. "But, look, let's not talk to Christina and Noelle about this whole thing, okay? I don't want to gross them out with my illness while they're trying to enjoy their dessert—especially Noelle; she's got such a sweet tooth. It would suck if I ruined the one treat she enjoys every week."

"Totally," I said. It just felt really good to have *someone* on my side, finally. "I won't tell."

"Promise?"

It seemed like a weird thing to promise. I don't know why, but for some reason I remembered a girl at Loveland, Kim, who'd tried to tell Dionne and me about these laxatives she'd bought from the pharmacy, and how great they worked to help take the weight off. Dionne and I both thought that was pretty gross, and then Kim begged us not to say anything to our coach. As if we'd want to talk about bowel movements in any form, especially premeditated diarrhea, which seemed awful.

So I didn't know why I would want to talk about Jessie's puking in the first place, but I would've said just about anything at that moment to keep her almost-friendship. "Promise."

Six

"**O**kay, girls," Mo said after we'd finished our morning stretches. "Line up at edge of floor. Tallest to smallest."

We'd gotten the day before off—our one free day of the week, but now it was Monday and time to work again. Even that one day off was enough to make me feel extra achy and a little out of it. Sometimes, with gymnastics, the best thing to do is power through it. You'll hurt *somewhere* every day, but at least you won't have time to stop and think about it.

In a way, it had been nice to have a day away from the drama at the gym, but Dionne hadn't been around any of the times I'd called, and my mom had had to go in to the day care for some inventory thing. The day went by really slowly, and by the end of it I found myself craving interaction of any kind, even if it meant hanging around people like Christina, who hated me. I must be nuts.

Now, luckily, I was as far from Christina as possible, since she was the tallest of the four of us and I was the shortest, so I didn't have to intercept her dagger glares. Having to line up in order of height made no sense to me, but I fell into line anyway. I swear it was just a way to bring attention to the fact that I was still a good three inches shorter than Noelle, who was the second smallest after me. Whatever.

For a few moments, Mo just looked at all of us, her eyes sliding from one girl to the next. When she got to me, I resisted the urge to stick out my tongue.

"Elite qualifier is in one month," Mo said. Cheng came to stand next to her, his eyes on the blue floor mat as he nodded. This must have been important, because the only time we usually saw Cheng was during bars and vault practice, or when we ran through tumbling passes on the floor. I got the impression he did a lot more behind-the-scenes stuff than Mo did and was busier.

"Britt and Noelle, you do not have to qualify," Mo continued. "But you need to get ready for the Classic and Nationals, which are coming up in next few months. So I want half routines, with increased numbers. Understand?"

I said that I didn't, for once not because I was trying to be funny or clever. I really didn't understand. At my old gym, we'd trained competitively, of course, but I'd never been given this kind of structure.

Mo explained what Noelle and I were supposed to do. She wanted ten flawless first halves for our beam routines, followed by ten flawless second halves. Then we would be expected to stick three beam dismounts and to do five first and second halves on bars, both perfectly, with three stuck bars dismounts. On floor, we were to do one routine focusing on our dance, with simple layouts for our tumbling passes, except for our big last pass, which would be practiced in the pit. Then we'd do one full routine with connection passes on floor and our big final pass in the pit. As if that wasn't enough, we were also supposed to do twenty competitive vaults.

That would be our practice schedule for the next four weeks.

"We will be giving more attention to Jessie and Christina," Mo said, "but that does not mean that you can rest."

No kidding. The only thing that kept this place from being a sweatshop was that we didn't make anything. But if nasty rips on our palms and sore hamstrings could somehow be packaged and sold, we'd have been in trouble.

"Jessie and Christina, you will also do twenty competitive vaults," Mo said. "But instead of half routines, you do full. Five on bars and beam and two on floor."

This time, it seemed like she looked at all of us at once. I don't know how that's possible, with us spread out the way we were, Christina on one end and me on the other, but she did it. It felt like there was no escaping those intense black eyes.

"No falls," she said. "Only perfection counts."

"Yes, Coach Mo," all the girls said in unison. I must have missed the memo about when to reply and when to keep my mouth shut.

Mo reminded the other girls about the extra ballet classes they were supposed to be taking once a week to hone their dance skills. My mother was all over me to sign up, too, but I just couldn't see the point of mincing around in a little skirt and waving my arms in the air. Who needed grace when you had raw power?

"We also need to be more careful with eating," Mo said. "Eat healthy, but do not starve yourselves. You need energy. Understand?"

Out of the corner of my eye, I glanced at Jessie, on the other side of Noelle. I don't know what I expected—a flicker or a nervous tick, *something* to show how she felt about the subject of food—but she just faced forward, saying, "Yes, Coach Mo," with the rest of the girls.

"Britt?"

I turned my eyes back to Mo. "Yeah?"

"Do you understand?"

Why was I being singled out? "Yes, Coach Mo," I said.

She nodded curtly. "Good. You and Noelle, go to vault with Cheng. Jessie and Christina, you come with me to beam."

It was the first time we'd been split up, and it was a little weird. I mean, not that I was complaining. Having to deal with only one girl was way better than having to deal with three of them. But still. Jessie was my only real friend on the team.

Without saying a word (of course), Cheng crossed over to stand by the vaulting table. Noelle and I went to the chalk bowl and started rubbing the dry white powder on our hands and feet. You could always tell where gymnasts had started on the runway by the white circle they left behind.

When I was five years old and too young to need the chalk, I used to think it was the coolest part of gymnastics. Before my grandmother started teaching me at home, I used to go to school and run my fingers along the rim of the blackboard, applying the chalk dust carefully to my hands. My teachers hated when I did that.

Of course, our chalk is totally different—it's this powdery magnesium stuff, instead of the hard chalk that used to scratch against the blackboard. And it serves its purpose. Without it, my hands would be slick from sweat and would slide right off the bars or vault or beam. It would be superdangerous. But it also completely dries out my hands, making my skin peel off like layers of an onion.

"So . . ." I said, trying to think of something to say. I once saw a commercial where all these people working in an office are trying to make awkward conversation over the water cooler, but it just isn't happening. The chalk bowl is like the water cooler of the gymnastics world.

It was pointless, anyway. Noelle was staring at Scott, who was practicing a front handspring to three front layouts on the floor.

"That's easy," I said, following her gaze. "I could do that in my sleep. I thought he was practically a college gymnast."

She flushed, as though I'd just insulted *her*. "Maybe he's just warming up," she said. "Ever think of that?"

"Well, if he's going to warm up front hand-springs, he could at least do them right. His knees are bent."

"You're one to talk," Noelle muttered.

"What?" I asked, even though I'd totally heard her.

"Nothing," she said. Just as I'd thought. Noelle was a coward. Without her ringleader, Christina, around, she didn't know what to say or do. In my book, that was way worse than a sloppy front hand-spring.

I decided to try to make amends, though. It

wasn't like I needed any more enemies at the gym, and I still felt bad about the stuffed-animal incident with Noelle. I searched for some small talk that might make her open up. "So, he competes for his high school team?"

Noelle nodded, a dreamy expression on her face. "Did you know that he's already been accepted to Conner University with a full gymnastics scholarship?"

I remembered Mo's mentioning something like that, but since I hadn't gotten my copy of Scottie-the-Hottie Trivia, I hadn't known the name of the college. "Cool," I said. "Where's Conner?"

Noelle reddened. "It's only in Houston," she pointed out. "It's not that far away."

I was about to point out that I'd never said it was when I realized that Noelle was just supersensitive about the idea of never seeing Scott again. It seemed to me that she already had a long-distance relationship with him when he was practicing twenty feet away. How do you measure the distance of *not going to happen*?

Down by the vaulting table, Cheng stuck his fingers in his mouth and whistled. It was startling, not just because, hello, it was a piercing whistle, but because Cheng had actually made a sound. Would wonders never cease?

"You go first," Noelle said uncharitably.

"Fine," I said. I took my place about sixty feet down the runway. A lot of gymnasts like to start farther back—the runway is just around eighty feet long—but I don't need that much room. My legs are so short that those extra twenty feet make me feel like I'm running a marathon.

Well, that might be exaggerating. But I get a little bored running.

I sprinted down the runway, hurdling into a round-off onto the springboard. I propelled myself backward onto the vaulting table, my hands hitting squarely as I performed a single layout into a pit just like the one we used for floor. Vault timers, we call these. They're just for warm-up.

Cheng nodded, so I guessed it was okay. I started walking back to my place at the end of the runway, Noelle whooshing past me as she ran toward the vault. I didn't bother to glance back to see how she did. Of course, it was going to be perfect. Noelle's vaults always were.

After a few more vault timers each, Noelle and I were ready to work on our competitive vaults. We were both doing a Yurchenko one-and-a-half twist for our first vault, so basically, we just had to add the twists to the layout. Easy, right?

I couldn't even imagine what kinds of vaults people had done before Natalia Yurchenko came up with pretty much the coolest one ever. Now almost everyone does Yurchenko vaults. The move consists of a round-off onto a springboard, so that when you hit the vault table, you're facing backward. It totally revolutionized vaulting, and it all happened way back before I was born, which means I've never known a world without such an awesome skill.

On my first vault, I completely sat down. It felt as if I'd landed on the very edge of my heels, and my feet slipped right out from underneath me, until I was sitting on the mat. The worst part of it was that I couldn't count it toward my twenty vaults. I'd probably still be vaulting ten years after all the other girls were done.

As Noelle did her vault (stuck landing, what else?), I watched Jessie and Christina on the beam. Christina was already working on the second half of her beam routine, flowing through the leaps and acrobatic skills like she was on a beam four feet wide instead of four inches. Jessie was still on the first half, jumping down from the beam after a wobbly sheep jump, her landing totally blind as she kicked both legs up behind her until her toes touched the bottom of her red ponytail. She'd have to start over.

Jessie got back up on the beam, but she leaned too far forward and ended up having to jump to the mat on the other side. She blew her bangs out of her eyes, muttering something to herself as she climbed back up. I saw her check her balance one more time before continuing her routine. What was with her?

"Hey," I said as Noelle joined me at the end of the runway.

"What?" Noelle asked, but her eyes were on Scott, who was doing a scale at the corner of the floor mat.

I wanted to ask her if she thought Jessie was okay. I wanted to ask her if she'd noticed anything weird, like the way that Jessie picked at her food during snack or skipped it entirely, or the way that she disappeared sometimes into the bathroom. But I didn't know how to ask without her having some questions of her own, like what I was talking about or why I cared. And besides, I'd promised not to tell.

"Nothing," I said. "Don't worry about it."

When I got home, my grandmother was waiting, ready to discuss the part of *To Kill a Mockingbird* that I was supposed to read, where Jem and Scout mess with this weirdo who lives across the street, Boo Radley. They come up with this awesome game where they playact what they imagine he'd be like, making him crazier and crazier in every incarnation.

My grandmother gestured for me to take a seat, and I plopped down at the kitchen table, dropping my gym bag at my feet.

"Why do you think Atticus isn't happy about Jem and Scout's game?" she asked.

Because he was an adult, and adults never like seeing kids have fun. I wanted to say that, but I knew my grandmother would just ask me to elaborate, and then I'd have to defend it, when really I just liked to complain sometimes for no reason. So I decided to take the question at face value and respond to it the way I knew she wanted me to.

"Because they shouldn't be making fun of

Boo Radley," I said. "He hasn't done anything to them."

My grandmother beamed her approval, making some notation in her copy of the book. She encouraged me to write in mine, too, but that seemed like a horrible way to treat a nice hardcover book. *Engage the text*, she would say, but I don't go scribbling all over clothes my mother buys me, either, so it seemed like a wasteful thing to do.

"How could they turn their playacting into something more positive?"

My grandmother loved to do this, tie fictional characters up in knots and ask you how you would untie them. I always wanted to say, like, *I don't know, they're not real people. So they can't do anything.*

This time, though, I really didn't know what my grandmother wanted me to say. I shrugged. "They could join the school drama club?" I offered. "I don't know."

She considered that answer, pursing her lips and tilting her head first to one side, then the other, as though weighing whether it were right or wrong. "Interesting," she said. "I'm not sure their school would have a drama club. But what I meant was that they could imagine how Boo Radley might *feel*—

being an outcast—instead of vilifying him further. Does that make sense?"

Of course it did. I found myself wishing that the other girls at the gym would imagine how I might feel, being a new girl in a highly competitive gym, with no way to make friends at school or anywhere else. But then again, I also sympathized with the kids in the book, who were just trying to have fun with their little games. It was kind of like the way I had wanted to liven things up with my prank on Noelle, but instead wound up doing something that made everyone jump down my throat.

So the question wasn't whether I understood the stupid book or not. The question was whether, in comparison with the characters, I was the one trying to have fun but getting shut down or I was the misfit. Was I the Boo Radley of the Texas Twisters?

Seven

My mom called the gym to say she was running late that day after practice. I was surprised when Jessie invited me over to her house. "Your mom can pick you up from there," she said. "Come on, it'll be fun."

Jessie's house was in a gated community where all the houses had big columns in front and were painted in variations on the same three yellows, pinks, and beiges. Compared to my small brown ranch house with its huge prickly hedges in front, it looked like a palace.

Jessie led me through the front foyer and the

stuffy-looking living room ("We never use this; it's just for when my grandparents come.") to a large kitchen. A teenage girl with long blond hair was chatting on a cell phone.

"I know, right?" the girl was saying. "You get it; I don't know why Jake doesn't. He is *such* a jerk. Do you know that he—"

She spun around and saw Jessie and me staring at her, then rolled her eyes. "Sorry," she said to the person on the other end of the line as she disappeared behind a door into a bedroom, "I can never get any *privacy* here."

"My stepsister, Tiffany," Jessie explained. "She thinks the world revolves around lip gloss. Come on, I'll show you my room."

Jessie's room had to be as big as the rest of the house, and it was a masterpiece of messiness. I saw what the other girls had been teasing her about on my first day at gym. She had more clothes than I'd ever owned in my life, strewn about every surface of the room, and there was just *stuff* everywhere. As I crossed over to her bed, I stepped on a Minnie Mouse Pez dispenser, nearly slipped on a piece of notebook paper with doodles all over it, and had to move a Scrabble board over to clear a place to sit.

"So," I said, "what do you want to do?" I was very aware that Jessie was my only quasi friend in Texas so far, and I was afraid to mess everything up by suggesting something babyish like painting each other's nails. Not that nail polish was allowed at Texas Twisters—at least, other than the clear kind, and, if it's not a color, what's the point?

"I have a bunch of old gymnastics competitions saved on my DVR. Want to watch those?"

She was already selecting last year's American Invitational from her list, so I figured she didn't need me to reply.

The first few minutes were filled with all that stupid commentating the announcers do—here's the girl to beat, blah blah blah, but look out for young hopeful so-and-so, the ultimate rivalry, and all that—and so I pushed the rest of the stuff off Jessie's bed to stretch out, propping my chin in my hands. "Do you have any other brothers or sisters?"

"Just Tiffany, who's fifteen, and Josh, my seventeen-year-old stepbrother."

"I always wanted to have a sister," I said. "Or a brother. You know, someone to hang around with when my parents weren't home."

Jessie laughed. "Count yourself lucky. I used to have it sweet when it was only me, but then Mom married Rick, and they came with the deal. I barely hang around with Rick's kids at all."

I guess it's not the same when they're not related to you, because then there's no rule saying they have to love you no matter what.

"I am so jealous of her," Jessie sighed; for a second I thought she was talking about Tiffany. But then I saw the gymnast on the screen, dancing around the floor mat on the balls of her feet as if she had all the energy in the world.

"Yeah, she's good. She ends up winning, right?"

"Of course," Jessie said. "She always wins. You can tell just by looking at her."

There was a close-up of the gymnast's face, and I squinted, trying to see whatever elusive superiority might exist in her features. Her nose was kind of pointy, her eyebrows were way too plucked, and her hair was pulled back so tightly it gave me a headache just to look at it. "She does look kind of smug," I agreed.

Jessie had turned her desk chair around and was straddling it with her arms resting on the back. She shook her head. "She looks smug because she wins. But she wins because she's thin."

Something about the way Jessie said it sent shivers down my spine. It was almost like she'd said it many times before, even if never out loud.

"I wish I was taller, like you," I said, "and had more muscle. That's what's really important—imagine if your arms looked like twigs. They'd snap in half if you tried to do a back handspring!"

I expected her to laugh, but she simply kept watching as the gymnast on television flipped her way through her last tumbling pass. "It's just scientific," she said.

"Right. Science says twigs and gymnastics are not a good combination. It *is* scientific."

The score flashed on the screen. With a high difficulty level and nearly perfect execution, it was hard to deny that she was the best.

"See, it pays to be little," Jessie went on. "Like you—your routines are harder than mine, and yet you barely break a sweat. If I tried the same thing, I'd have to work twice as hard just to get my body to rotate all the way around."

"I'm also shorter," I said. "Christina is tall and skinny, and she can't do all the hard stuff, either."

"That's because she doesn't want to."

When Christina had been crying over her failure to do a full-in, it had seemed as if she wanted to pretty badly, although now that Jessie mentioned it, I did wonder what motivated her. The other girls had more obvious reasons for being involved in such a demanding sport. Noelle's mom had been a gymnast, so maybe Noelle wanted to follow in her footsteps. Jessie had told me that after her parents got divorced and her mom remarried, she'd latched on to gymnastics as something to make her special, to help her stand out in a house that was filling up with other people. I didn't love the strict regime of workouts, but it was all worth it for that feeling I got as I was flying over the bars, or propelling my body through the air with a single push against the vaulting table. Christina was an only child; I doubted that her mother, with her perfect hair, had ever been an athlete, and Christina didn't seem to relish the adrenaline rush of gymnastics the way I did. So, what was her story?

Another gymnast on the screen slipped off the bars and belly-flopped onto the mat below. It was obvious she wasn't really a contender, though, since they didn't bother to show any of her other routines, just the one where she face-planted it. That's why I planned to be the best gymnast ever by the time I made it to a televised meet. At least if I messed up one routine, I'd still have the other three to show my grandkids someday.

There was a knock at the door, and Jessie's mom poked her head into the room. Her carrot-red hair was pulled back in a French braid, and her cheeks puffed out a little like a chipmunk's when she smiled.

"I'm Britt," I reminded her. "I'm new at the gym."

"Of course, I met you at the team yogurt outing. And Jessie's told me all about you." She chipmunk beamed at me. I wondered what Jessie had told her. "Jess, honey, have you finished your homework?"

"Most of it," Jessie mumbled.

"I'm sorry?"

"I said I'm doing it," Jessie replied in a louder voice; her mom raised her eyebrows as she shut the door.

"Want me to rewind?" Jessie asked after her mom had left. I shook my head, since we'd only missed a routine that hadn't looked very interesting anyway. I mean, it was the American Invitational, and this girl was doing a side somi on the beam, which basically looked like an aerial cartwheel with ugly tucked legs and flexed feet. Why didn't she just yank some other moves from her compulsory Level Five routine and throw those in while she was at it?

I shared my opinion with Jessie, but she said that the side somi was "acrobatic" and part of the "presentation." It was so nice to chat about gymnastics without its being about weight that I immediately reversed my opinion, and we rewound the tape so we could analyze the way simple skills could add elegance to a routine.

"What do you have to do for homework?" I asked. "Maybe I could help."

"Nah, it's eighth grade stuff. Algebra."

"I can do that. My grandma taught me."

It wasn't like homework was my favorite thing in the world, either. But I was determined to make Jessie see how awesome a friend I could be, and this seemed as good a way to do it as any.

At first, Jessie looked at me as if I'd just suggested doing a balance-beam routine over an ocean filled with piranhas, but eventually she reached into her backpack and pulled out a glossy orange textbook. I turned it over in my hands.

"So this is what it's like being in public school, huh?" I said. "I do a lot of stuff out of workbooks and from stuff my grandma gets online."

There were a whole bunch of names written on the inside cover of the book, ending with Jessie's name, written in big, bubbly handwriting with a purple pen. I flipped through the book and saw at least one obscene word that was not written in purple pen, so I figured Jessie wasn't the vandal. My money was on the kid two names above hers, Justinn Myers. I'd act out, too, if my parents had saddled me with a random extra letter at the end of my name.

"We all go to the public school," Jessie said. "Our parents agreed we should have normal lives outside of gymnastics, even though we take the first period off to practice and eat grilled-chicken salads for lunch instead of pizza like everyone else. But I guess it's better than being totally isolated." She glanced at me. "No offense."

"Well . . ." I didn't know what to say. Being homeschooled could feel very lonely, considering that it was just me and my grandmother, so I couldn't seriously be offended by Jessie's comment.

And yet it still kind of stung. "So let's see what chapter you're on," I said instead.

One of the homework problems was to illustrate the equation $2x - 10 = x + 1$ with a real-life problem. "All you really have to do is figure out what you want x to stand for," I said, "and then fill in the blanks."

"Okay," Jessie said. "I weigh twice as much as I want to, and so I'll lose ten pounds. Whereas you weigh exactly as much as you want to, and you could gain one. Does that work?"

It didn't on so many levels, but where would I even begin? "If that were really true, your ideal weight would be, like, fifty pounds or something," I said. "That's just sick."

Jessie scowled, snatching the textbook back from me. "Obviously, I'm not being *literal*," she said. "I thought the point was just to come up with stuff for the numbers to stand for. You never told me it had to actually make any sense."

I didn't want to pick a fight, so instead I just focused on the part of her equation that didn't work, the part that could be better explained.

"We can't be the same variable," I said. "The x can't stand for both you and me."

But in some ways, wouldn't it have been easier if it could've? If I could somehow have been Jessie, and known the secret to earning Christina's and Noelle's friendship, and had a mother who cared enough to come to the gym at least *sometimes*? And then Jessie could have been me, and known what it was like to be scared—terrified that I'd never fit in, and worried that the only friend I had was dealing with something much bigger than I could ever handle.

That night, when I got home after my mom finally picked me up, I locked myself in the bathroom. I stood on the edge of the bathtub so I could see all of my body reflected in the mirror.

Everything looked familiar. My blond hair with its wisps around my face, that wouldn't be restrained by any clips. My eyes that I had used to wish were blue-green, but that were just blue. My strong shoulders, my arms that looked normal under a T-shirt but that I knew were made of muscle and sinew and could spin me around the high bar in twenty giant swings in a row. My narrow hips, my short legs, my feet that were always too dry from all the chalk I used, so they didn't look cute in flip-flops.

I stared at the girl staring back at me, until the image started to warp and become the reflection of a stranger. I wondered if that was what Jessie saw when she looked at herself in the mirror—although maybe she didn't have to try so hard to see it.

Eight

We were split up again at the next morning's practice, so I didn't really get to talk to Jessie. Noelle and I spent the whole time on vault. And then, when it was over, the other girls retreated to the locker room to shower before school. Since my grandmother was coming later to pick me up and take me home for my own schooling, I didn't need to worry about it. So what if I felt isolated sometimes? I also got to take a shower in the middle of history if I wanted to. I reminded myself to tell Jessie this, the next time she talked about homeschooling.

But I hated to be left out, so I joined the girls in

the locker room anyway. I just packed and unpacked my gym bag, trying to seem busy as I listened to the conversations behind the shower curtains.

"Sucks to be you, Noelle," Christina said, from stall number one. "Vault is the *worst*."

"I think it's kind of fun," I said, both because I liked to argue with Christina and because I wanted to make my presence known. It wasn't clear if Christina had been addressing Noelle in order to make a point of ignoring me (a total possibility) or because she thought I'd already left (also a possibility). Normally, I might've waited her out, interested in hearing whatever she might say behind my back. This time, I didn't feel up to that.

"*You* would," Christina said, as if having an affinity for vault were right up there with wanting to harm small animals.

Noelle's voice was barely audible over the sound of water streaming slowly but steadily from the faucets. "I don't mind vault."

"You don't mind anything," Christina said, and somehow she made that, too, sound right up there with serial murder. "That's your problem."

"Speaking of problems," I said, "how's that tucked full-in coming along?"

I tried to make my tone as friendly as possible, but I wasn't surprised when Christina peeked out from behind the shower curtain. Her face was dripping wet, and her black hair was plastered to her head. Her less than perfect look took a little of the steam out of her angry glare.

"Shut up," she said.

"Fine," I said. "Don't listen to me. But I'm telling you, it's all in your back handspring."

Christina made a face at me. "I've been doing back handsprings practically since I could walk. I sincerely *doubt* it has anything to do with that."

"Okay," I said in my best bored voice. This was the same voice I used on my mom a lot when she would talk about the arts and crafts she did with the four-year-olds. Like, who cares? It was either Popsicle sticks and glue or cotton balls and glue. Sometimes, it was Popsicle sticks, cotton balls, *and* glue. That was when it got semi-interesting.

"All right, Coach Brittany," Christina said, disappearing behind the curtain again. "Let's hear it. What's wrong with my handspring?"

"Nothing," I said, "for a double twist or a double tuck or whatever. But a tucked full-in is a double flip *with* a twist. It needs more power. You have to get stronger right from your round-off and snap your feet under your body. Right now, your feet are too far behind, and you don't get the height."

"Well, thanks for the insight," Christina said, "but I'll go ahead and wait for what the *real* coaches have to say, if it's all the same to you."

"You do that," I said, shrugging, even though she couldn't see me, "and continue to wipe out. It *is* all the same to me."

I saw Jessie's hand groping for the towel that was hanging on a hook just outside the shower, and I reached over to hand it to her. "Thanks," she said when she finally emerged, the towel wrapped around her like a strapless dress.

"How was practice today?" I asked. "I hate it when they split us up."

She shrugged. "Fine. Same as usual."

"Do you think you'll be ready for the qualifier?"

"Hmm?" Jessie brushed out her red hair, and I repeated the question. "Oh," she said. "Yeah, I'm sure it'll be fine."

She packed up her bag and retreated into one of the stalls to get changed. Noelle and Christina had already put on their sports bras in the main area and were now sliding shirts over their heads.

I wanted to ask Christina if anything had happened during practice to make Jessie so distracted, but I knew she'd just roll her eyes and tell me to mind my own business. I wanted to ask Noelle if she was aware of anything, but she'd been with me the whole morning.

"We'd better head out if we want to make third period," Noelle said.

"Hey, Jessie, are you riding with us?" Christina called through the stall door.

It swung open, and Jessie stepped out. "Of course," she said, and then she glanced at me. "Oh— Thanks for the help with my algebra homework, Britt. See you!"

And then somehow I was alone in the locker room, clammy with steam from other people's showers. It occurred to me that in the future I should take a shower, too, even though I could totally take one in the comfort of my own home, with the new showerhead my dad had put in that was supposed to make it feel like rain, and with my mom's fruity-smelling shampoo. Right now, the fact that I was the only one who didn't shower there just made one more way I was different from everyone else in this new gym. I wore beam shoes;

I was homeschooled; I wasn't invited to sleepovers. I was Boo Radley.

Normally, I wasn't the kind of person who wanted to be like everyone else. In fact, I liked being a little quirky. Dionne had always said that the thing she liked best about me was the way I could make her laugh, and that she never knew what I would say or do next.

So far, though, Texas didn't seem to like quirky.

"What do you think that means?"

It was probably the third time my grandmother had asked, but I wasn't listening. Instead of following along with her discussion of *To Kill a Mockingbird*, I was doodling stick figures flipping on a beam I had drawn along the edge of my notebook page. For now, they were just doing simple layouts. It turned out that drawing a full twist was just as hard as doing one.

"You know," I said, "Jessie told me that they don't read *To Kill a Mockingbird* until ninth grade."

I knew Grandma must have been getting impatient, but she didn't let on. That was one of the best things about her. "Is that right?"

"Uh-huh," I said. "She's in eighth grade. She

said that it's on the reading list for next year, when she gets to high school. She said it was crazy that I was learning it now."

"Do *you* think it's crazy?"

I should've anticipated that question. Another of my grandmother's not-so-secret weapons is turning a question around so that you're forced to actually think about something. It can get really annoying.

"I don't know," I said. "It's just that there's a lot of other stuff going on right now. If I have to try to understand this supertough book, too, my head may explode."

"That's unfortunate," Grandma said, but she just tilted her book to let me see the part she'd underlined. "It's in the third chapter," she said. "Atticus tells Scout that you can never fully understand someone until you climb into his skin and walk around in it. What does that mean to you?"

"I don't know," I said. "Sounds kind of gross, walking around in someone's skin. Like Buffalo Bill in that really creepy movie about the serial killer. You know, the one who makes dresses out of people's skin?"

Grandma closed her book in exasperation.

"How in the world did you even see that kind of thing?"

I shrugged. "Late-night television."

"So, you're telling me that if I showed you the movie *To Kill a Mockingbird*, maybe you'd pay attention?"

Just the mention of a movie made me perk up a bit. "So there is one? Sweet. Let's order it."

"Settle down, Miss Brittany Lee," Grandma said. My voice had been rising, and since my dad was sleeping upstairs after a late-night shift at the restaurant, I had to keep my voice low. "There's no serial killer in the movie, either. Let's focus on the book for now. Remember what we talked about last time. What do you think Atticus means when he tells Scout that you have to walk in someone's skin to understand them?"

"I guess, just that . . ." I colored in the heads of my stick figures until they were completely filled with blue ink. "Like, you have to see where people are coming from."

"Good," Grandma said. "Can you give me an example?"

"Well, at gym, my friend Jessie . . ." I stopped, glancing at my grandmother.

"Go on."

By now, I'd punched a hole in the head of one of my figures with my ballpoint pen. It looked as if some stick person had lost her head in mid-handspring. "I don't know," I said. "It's weird. She thinks she's fat or something, and she always obsesses about food and losing weight."

"And what do you think?"

"I think she looks like one of these people," I said, holding up my stick-figure drawings. But I couldn't keep a straight face, and I broke into a grin. "Not really, that would be scary. But she's totally fine. I mean, maybe she could eat healthier or whatever, but I think she shouldn't worry about it so much."

"Try to put yourself in her place," Grandma said, "the way Atticus says to do. What do you think she might be feeling?"

My grandmother is a huge fan of these assignments, where you learn something from a book but you also learn something about yourself. "Um, she's scared?"

"Scared," Grandma repeated, but not as if she was questioning it—more like she wanted to turn it over in her mind a little bit. "That's an interesting choice of words. Why do you think she's scared?"

"Because," I said, "she hasn't made it to Elite yet, and Noelle and I have. Christina's definitely got what it takes, if she can just up her difficulty. But Jessie's different. Things come slower for her."

"So, why do you think that would make her scared about her weight?"

"Well, I mean, it's true that less weight makes you flip faster and jump higher. Noelle is on the shorter side, like me, and we're both pretty tiny. Christina is the tallest, but she's naturally really skinny. Jessie's just got more muscle, that's all."

My grandmother nodded. One major benefit to being homeschooled is that I can bring up gymnastics examples all I want, and I'm never shut down or mocked by classmates. Dionne told me once that she felt like a freak show being in public school, where people treated her as if she was from a completely different universe. Sometimes I wanted to go to regular school, just to see what it would be like, but I also liked the fact that I could say whatever I wanted to with my grandmother. She doesn't mind that I live on Planet Gymnastics all the time.

"Putting yourself in Jessie's skin, what do you think she needs right now?"

Personally, I thought she could use a big, juicy

hamburger, but I knew that wasn't the answer my grandmother was looking for. I was about to respond when I heard the front door slam and the slap of my mom's work flats on the tiled floor.

"Hello, Pamela," Grandma said. "You're home early."

It was kind of weird, actually. At two thirty in the afternoon, my mom should definitely have been watching the rug rats at her day care center; it was prime time, when all the younger kids were waking up from their postlunch naps and all the older kids were starting to trickle in from school.

"Yeah," I said. "Why are you here?"

"Ah, just the way a mother likes to be greeted," my mother said ruefully, pressing a kiss on the top of my head. "Hello, Asta. Good lesson today?"

"We were just discussing *To Kill a Mockingbird*," my grandmother said, glancing at me, "and the importance of empathy."

I didn't remember that word being thrown around, but I nodded anyway. "So, what's up?"

It was only then that I realized my mother was seriously glowing. Like, she was practically *radiating* all over me. I'd never seen her that happy.

"Well," she said, the words coming out in a rush,

"Debbie—you know, the woman who owns the center?—is looking to sell. I told her I'd definitely be interested, so we were talking about drawing up some documents to have the licenses transferred this week. Isn't that exciting?"

Owning a business consisting of a bunch of screaming kids? Wow, someone needed to work on her definition of "exciting."

"Yeah," I said. "Totally."

"That's great, Pamela," Grandma said, and obviously she'd drunk the Kool-Aid, because she seemed to mean it. "It's what you've always wanted."

"I know!" my mom said. "It's going to be great. I just came home for a few minutes to pick up some of the financial stuff we need to go over after work, but then I'm heading back in time for an after-school snack. So I'll be out of your hair!"

I rolled my eyes. Like *that* was my problem.

"That's fine," Grandma said. "Congratulations again."

My mom turned to me. "I was hoping to repaint the classrooms at some point. Maybe one Sunday, when you girls are off practice. What do you think? Would you all like to come out and have a paint-and-pizza party?"

It was weird the way she said "girls." Like we were all such close friends and she saw the four of us as inseparable, when nothing could have been further from the truth. "Mom, we're not supposed to have pizza," I said. "Remember? Our bodies are our temples and all that?"

"Well, when your father finally gets a night off, I'm sure he can make us something *healthy* for a celebratory dinner. I know it'll be tough to arrange, with all of our schedules."

And about to get tougher still, if my guess was right. But I didn't want to seem like a total brat, so I forced a smile. "Yeah," I said. "Sounds awesome."

My mother let out one last strange, giddy laugh before disappearing into her bedroom. If I ever get that jazzed about owning a place where you basically change dirty diapers all day, someone shoot me.

"Well, that's exciting," Grandma said.

That was the buzzword of the day, apparently. "Yeah."

She looked at me for a moment; the skin around her eyes didn't crinkle like it usually did. "Where were we?" she asked quietly.

It wasn't as if I had short-term memory loss.

I knew *exactly* where we'd left off. I just didn't feel like pursuing it, in case Grandma wanted me to project myself into my mother's skin or something.

"I don't know," I said. "But I have to go to gym in, like, half an hour. Can't we move on to social studies?"

I half expected her to protest, but she nodded. "Fine," she said. "Open your American History book where we left off, about the industrial revolution."

I did as she told me, sliding *To Kill a Mockingbird* under the coffee table. If she'd insisted, I could definitely have answered her question before my mom came home. *What do you think Jessie needs right now?*

I thought Jessie needed a friend like Atticus Finch, someone who could be strong and do what was right, no matter what the consequences. But then I remembered the promise I'd made to Jessie, and the one glaring thing I'd neglected to tell my grandmother. I wondered if I was up to the task.

Nine

That afternoon at practice, I tried to find a way to bring up the painting, but I couldn't seem to find a good time. It didn't help that I was still conflicted about the answer I was hoping for. I dreaded their saying yes; I also feared their saying no.

As it turned out, Christina approached me first, at the water fountain during a break. "Look," she said. "I'm not happy about this, so I'm just going to say it."

I waited, too stunned to speak.

She rolled her eyes. "Willyoucometomysleep-overSaturday?"

"What?"

I saw her clench her jaw. She obviously thought I was just being difficult. "Will. You. Come. To. My. Sleepover. Saturday."

"Oh," I said. "I'd love to."

I was pretty impressed with how cool I'd been about the whole thing. I leaned down to get a sip of water, but Christina's hand shot out to cover the water fountain button.

"You know that my mom is making me ask you, right? It was supposed to be just me, Noelle, and Jessie."

"I know," I said.

"But—" Christina shook her head. "Then why would you agree to come? Wouldn't you just feel . . . unwelcome?"

"I know you'll try to make me feel unwelcome," I said, "but the sleepover sounds like fun, and I'm happy to be invited. So, thank you. Yes, I'll be there."

She continued to stare at me until I gently reached under her hand to depress the button, sending a clear stream of water shooting toward my mouth. It tasted more refreshing than any water I remembered drinking.

"So, Saturday night," I said, when I'd filled my

water bottle and was heading back to the floor, "should be fun. And Sunday, my mom asked if we could help her paint her new day care, so this will be perfect—we can all just head over there together."

"Sounds . . . perfect," Christina said. She looked as if she'd hit her head on the balance beam.

"Oh, yeah," I said. "We'll have a blast."

Of course, that night I had to call Dionne and try to hash out what I should wear and what I should bring and how I should act. I was asking her whether I should bring my Twister game when Dionne cleared her throat.

"What?" I asked, aware that she'd been silent for a while.

"It's just that . . . Do you remember when we played Twister at my birthday party last year?"

"Uh, yeah." That was why I was thinking about bringing it this time. Nothing got more competitive or more hilarious than a group of gymnasts in contortions trying to touch right hands to green and left legs to yellow. It had been the hit of Dionne's party.

"Well, I shouldn't say 'we.'" Dionne paused, as though she was carefully considering before deciding to go ahead. "*I* didn't really participate. In fact, I spent most of the night reading a book on my bed while you guys played."

I remembered now. I had thought it was really weird that Dionne would be so antisocial when it was her party. If she hadn't felt like playing Twister for any reason, she could always have offered to operate the spinner to see what configuration we'd have to get into next.

"So, what's your point?"

"You still don't know?" Dionne said. "Britt, it was *my* party. I wanted to watch movies and paint each other's nails and talk. Instead, you totally took it over with your game, turning it into this crazy competition."

I was stung by her words, especially because they were completely unfair. Dionne's party had been a dud. If I hadn't saved it with Twister, everyone would've watched some dumb movie about girls who were also mermaids or something and gone to bed by nine. Instead, I got it rocking. Everyone had been laughing and having a great time, gathered around the Twister board, while Dionne had pouted over in the corner. Now, she was saying it was because I somehow "took over" her party, although that was absolutely ridiculous. I'd just given it a much-needed makeover.

"What's your point?" I asked again, my voice tight.

Dionne sighed into the phone. "Look, that was a while ago," she said. "I'm not still mad. I'm just trying to say that you should watch yourself. Remember that this party is *not* the Brittany Show."

"The *Brittany Show*?"

"It's not—you know what I mean."

"Yeah," I said. "I guess I do." And then I pressed TALK on the phone to end the call, my finger pounding the spongy button with more force than was really necessary.

Dionne was the one who'd suggested I try a prank in the first place, and look at how that had turned out. Now she wanted me to play it safe? All because of something I'd done a year ago that had annoyed her and that she hadn't even told me about at the time?

It wasn't as if I made everything about me. It was just that some situations needed to be livened up, and that was kind of my specialty. And if there had ever been a group of girls that could have used my brand of fun, it was the Texas Twisters.

But then I had a brief flash of Jessie in that bathroom, her knees red from kneeling on the tile, and I wondered if "fun" would be enough. And I wondered if it could be too much, if it could mask something else that was going on—such as the fact that I'd never even noticed that Dionne was mad at her party, or that Jessie might starve herself until she was so thin that she could just slip through the cracks—all because we were too busy having fun to notice.

Ten

Christina's house had a curvy orange roof and white stucco walls. My mom called it Spanish-style.

"But Christina's from Mexico, not Spain," I said.

She laughed. "Oh, honey, it's just a style of architecture. Do you have everything? Your bathing suit?"

I had probably overpacked, but I wouldn't have put it past Christina to "forget" to tell me key details of the night, like that you were supposed to bring your own sleeping bag, or that you should have brought a swimsuit, since she had a pool. I didn't know if she had a pool, but I wasn't taking any chances. I didn't want to be sitting on a lounge chair talking to Mrs. Flores while everyone else played Marco Polo.

I gave my mom a kiss good-bye. She tugged at my sleeve before I got out of the car. "You did ask them about painting tomorrow, right? It's just that I really need to do it on a weekend when none of the little kids are there, and I'd like it to be sooner rather than later."

"Yeah, I told Christina. She said it sounded perfect." It was totally true. I hadn't *asked* Christina. I had told her, and that was exactly what she'd said. The only part I left out was that she was so shell-shocked when I said I was actually going to come to her sleepover that I doubted she'd even heard me.

"Great!" My mom smiled. "Well, have fun."

My duffel bag was so heavy I had to drag it up to the front door. Before I could ring the bell, it swung open to reveal Mrs. Flores, wearing a huge smile and an apron right out of a Betty Crocker commercial. Still, she managed to look stylish.

"Brittany! Come in, come in." She made a move to grab the duffel bag, but as soon as she tried to lift it and felt how heavy it was, she withdrew her hand.

"I would have driven you from gym, you know," she said as she led me into the kitchen. "All the other girls have been here for a couple of hours."

I'd thought about pushing my luck with that, but there were some last-minute things I'd needed to pack, anyway, like a comic book (in case I got bored), several extra changes of clothes (in case whatever I was wearing wasn't appropriate or got ruined because of some horrible prank), and a bottle of air freshener. I'd been purposely avoiding beans or anything else fart-producing for the past few days, but I didn't want to take any chances that there'd be some smell I'd want to cover up.

I'd left Twister at home. Not because I actually put any stock in what Dionne had said, but, you know, just in case.

As soon as I walked into Christina's room, everyone got silent. Christina was sitting on a huge, canopy bed with a frilly purple comforter on it, Noelle was at her feet with a forkful of speared shrimp suspended near her mouth, and Jessie sat on an uncomfortable-looking white stool in front of a vanity. I'd never actually seen a vanity in a real-life room before, only in catalogs and on TV. I definitely got the name—when a piece of furniture is basically one gigantic mirror, it's pretty obvious that its only purpose is to let people stare at themselves and think about how beautiful they are. Perfect for Christina.

It was hard to believe that in the last week I'd been in both Jessie's room and Christina's. I dragged my duffel bag over to a corner and plopped down on the floor next to it.

"So," I said, "what's up?"

Christina went back to flipping through an issue of *International Gymnast*, and Noelle chewed slowly, as though she preferred turning the same bite over in her mouth again and again to responding to me. Sometimes I thought Noelle was worse than Christina. Christina actively hated me, but it was hard to tell with Noelle—it seemed as though she was more interested in staying on Christina's good side than in actually speaking up for herself.

"Christina was about to start up Rock Band," Jessie said.

"Cool," I said. "I can be the drummer. My grandma thinks music is part of any well-rounded education, so I know all about different time signatures and stuff. My grandma says I can keep a mean beat."

"Did your grandma sew your outfit?" Christina asked, her gaze flicking up from the magazine.

I looked down at my capri pants and my T-shirt with sparkly turquoise polka dots on it. When I'd chosen these clothes to wear, I had thought they seemed cool—effortlessly casual, as if I couldn't have cared less what I wore but had somehow managed to pull it together anyway. But suddenly it felt like the stupidest outfit ever.

"My grandmother is an art historian," I said. "She doesn't make art, she just critiques it."

I thought that was a fitting response, but Christina's comeback was swift.

"Who called *that* art?"

The room was silent for a few moments. Surprisingly, it was Noelle who spoke up. "Can we not do this tonight?" she said. "Please? I'm all achy from practice, and I just want to chill out."

"I'm pretty sore, too," I said, seizing on that as a neutral conversation starter. Who doesn't like to compare scars? "Check out my hands. They're all ripped up."

I held out my palms for everyone to see. Weeks of constant friction against the bars and rubbing dry chalk into every crease made them look like parchment. I had a blister on one palm that refused to go away no matter how much cream I put on it.

Christina shrugged. "That's what you get for not wearing grips," she said.

Grips help support your wrists and have strips of leather that cover the palms of your hands. Some gymnasts use them; some gymnasts don't. Personally, I like to feel the full contact of the bar beneath my hands, even if it means I pay for it later.

"I don't wear grips," Noelle pointed out. "Neither do the Chinese gymnasts, who are some of the best bar workers in the world."

Christina was silent.

"Come on, let's play Rock Band," Jessie said.

Once we got into the game, it was surprisingly fun. Even Christina seemed to forget that she thought I was the scum of the earth, and we both laughed at Noelle's singing. As soon as Noelle realized you could get extra points by diva-ing out some parts of the song, she started yodeling and trilling all kinds of weird noises into the microphone. Every time *GREAT JOB!* flashed across the screen, I just about died.

"I'm still hungry," Christina said. "Who wants a Popsicle?"

Noelle and I both chimed in to say yes. Jessie just shook her head. "I'm okay," she said.

After Noelle and Christina left to get the Popsicles from the fridge, I glanced at Jessie. "There aren't many calories in Popsicles, you know," I said, trying to keep my voice casual. "It's basically flavored water."

"Oh, it's not that," she said. "I just don't really feel like it."

Christina brought back cherry for her, orange for Noelle, and grape for me. I tried to read some significance into the choice of flavors, but I couldn't. I liked grape, so who cared if somehow it was meant as a slight?

"I'm sick of Rock Band," Christina said. "Let's play something else instead."

Noelle stuck her tongue out and caught a drip of orange juice running down her Popsicle stick. "Can we play Super Mario Brothers?" she asked. "We could just take turns."

Christina smiled, her eyes sparkling devilishly. "I had something else in mind," she said. "What about Truth or Dare?"

I had heard about Truth or Dare before. Dionne said that mostly it was just people asking who you liked or daring you to tell someone's older brother you liked him. To me, that didn't sound as fun as Super Mario Brothers or even Twister, but I wasn't about to say so and look lame.

"I'm up for it," I said. "How do we start?"

"Well, since you seem to want to play so badly, why don't we start with you?" Christina said. She still had that look in her eyes that made me distrust her.

"Okay," I said. "Dare."

"Wait, we're not even doing it right," Noelle said. "We should all be sitting in a circle on the floor. And, Christina, you should put on some music so that your mom can't hear."

"Like she has nothing better to do than listen at my door," Christina said.

Noelle looked at her with raised eyebrows. "What about the time that you said you hated gymnastics and always had, and she burst out crying, until you had to tell her you were just joking?"

Christina flushed. "God, Noelle, save it for the game, why don't you?" But she got up and plugged her iPod in to the speakers on her nightstand, turning the volume down until I could just barely make out the sounds of the latest Miley Cyrus single.

Once we were all sitting cross-legged in a circle, Christina turned to me. "Okay, Britt, so, truth or dare?"

"Dare," I repeated.

"You can't do that," Christina said.

"What?"

"You can't pick dare this early on. Nobody picks dare. You have to do a few truths first."

That was the dumbest rule I'd ever heard. "Then why call it Truth or Dare? Why not call it Mostly Truth but a Little Dare Toward the End?"

Noelle giggled.

"It's not a *rule*," Jessie said. "Britt can pick dare if she wants to."

"Whatever. Fine. Let me just think of something."

The circle got quiet as they decided my fate. I listened to Miley's twang over some pulsing electronic beat and realized I'd probably have the song stuck in my head for days.

"Okay, I've got it." Christina squinted at me. "I dare Britt to . . . lick the toilet seat."

Jessie made a gagging noise. "Gross! Isn't it supposed to be a dare that you would do yourself?"

"Who says I wouldn't?"

"*Would* you?" Noelle asked.

Christina threw up her hands. "All right, you suggest something, then. This is already no fun."

I guessed that it wasn't the time to say that I would totally have licked the toilet seat if that were my dare. I mean, sure, it was disgusting, but I was okay with that. It was a *dare*. It was supposed to be horrible. And it wasn't like I couldn't wash my mouth out right afterward.

But at the same time, if I could get out of it, why not?

"What about a toilet-paper shirt?" Jessie said. "Britt has to wrap herself in toilet paper and wear the shirt for the rest of the game."

Everyone agreed that that was a way better idea, so we trooped into the bathroom to begin the process of making a toilet-paper shirt. Basically, it consisted of wrapping my torso up like a mummy and then winding the toilet paper around my arms. It was scary how good the shirt ended up looking. That's what you get with four girls who probably learned how to wrap an Ace bandage at the age of five.

Christina grabbed her digital camera and snapped some pictures of me as I hammed it up, standing with a hand on my hip and striking a diva pose, then sitting, with my chin resting on my fist, looking pensive. She laughed, but for once it didn't feel as if it was at me, so I didn't mind.

When we were back in the circle, Christina said it was my turn to ask the person next to me a question. Noelle picked truth, and I thought for a few moments, trying to figure out a good one.

"Why do you like Scott so much?" I asked finally.

I saw that the tips of Noelle's ears were turning bright red.

She picked at some fuzz on the carpet before looking up. "I don't know," she said. "I mean, he's cute."

Christina and Jessie laughed.

"Is that all?" I asked. "I mean, it can't be just those blue eyes, right?"

Noelle blushed even more, if that were possible. "No," she said, her voice low. "It's not just that. It's . . . everything. He's so nice, and mature. Not like the boys at school, who are always trying to snap girls' bras and stuff. And he's a serious gymnast. It's totally possible that he'll go to the next Olympics, and I'll be seventeen then. . . ."

She broke off, as though she'd said too much. "Of course, I would never dream of letting a relationship stand in the way of Olympic gold," she said stiffly.

I now knew my next question for Noelle: *If your only chance to be with Scott was during the Olympics, would you take it?* I already knew her answer—none of us would risk something as huge as an Olympic medal, no matter how cute the guy. But I was betting she'd hesitate for just a second, and that would be enough to tease her about later.

Not that the women's gymnastics team got to interact much with the men's team during the Olympics. The men often stayed in the Olympic Village, while the women's team had stayed off-site for the past three or four games. I guess the coaches didn't want people getting any ideas.

Jessie picked truth, too, and Noelle asked her what famous person she'd want to have lunch with. Boring!

"Nadia Comaneci," Jessie replied. "So I could ask her how she did it. Or maybe that cute guy from the cell phone commercial."

"So you could ask him what?" Christina asked snidely.

"How about asking him why he doesn't stop texting that girl with the braces and go out with one of us?" I put in.

"How about because he probably lives in California and has a supermodel girlfriend?" Christina returned, but with less venom. As if she wouldn't totally have dated that guy. Even I had to admit he was adorable, with a dimple in his cheek that showed every time he smiled down at his phone in the commercial.

After Christina had picked truth when it was her turn, Jessie glanced around the circle. Her eyes landed on me for just a second, and then she asked, "Christina, why don't you like Britt?"

I felt my pulse start racing, as though I was running laps around the floor mat. This was going to be interesting.

Christina looked at me for a long time, and I wondered if she was trying to figure out a nice way to phrase her reply or if she was trying to figure out the nastiest thing she could possibly say. But nothing could have prepared me for what she said when she did finally speak.

"Because she's better than me," she said.

I stared at her.

"Oh, come on," she said. "You know it. I know it. You're younger and shorter and way more obnoxious, but you have absolutely no fear. You can flip your body through the air and not worry about what's going to happen when you hit the ground. I'm not like that. I'm always a little scared."

"But that's not Britt's fault," Jessie pointed out.

"I know that," Christina snapped. "I answered the question, didn't I? No one can say I wasn't honest."

In a way, it was just as fearless of Christina to tell the truth as it was for me to do the tucked full-in on floor. I thought about saying so, but figured she would think I was teasing her.

Christina tossed her head impatiently. "So I get to ask the next question, right? Let's get to the juicy stuff. Britt, truth or dare?"

My dare last time hadn't actually been too bad, but I knew I had to pay my dues. "Truth," I said.

Christina leaned in as though it were only the two of us. "What's your biggest secret right now?" she asked.

I ran through all the possibilities in my head. Whenever my mom took me to the grocery store, I would grab a caramel from the candy bin and eat it while we shopped, even though I know you're supposed to put it one of the baggies and pay for it. Sometimes, if I was over at someone else's house and I had a booger, I wiped it under the table or on the wall. I worried that my mother didn't love me as much as she loved those kids at her day care.

And then, for some reason, I thought about *To Kill a Mockingbird*. And I thought about staring at myself in the mirror and trying to see what Jessie might see. And I thought about how the only thing lonelier than moving to a new place with no friends was carrying around a secret that was as big as the state of Texas.

I glanced at Jessie. Her eyes were wide and panicked, and I heard the words coming out of my mouth before I had a chance to think about them, or to will them back.

"I think Jessie might have an eating disorder," I said.

Eleven

Noelle spoke first. "Why would you say that?"

"It's just—" I stopped when Jessie stood up and rushed out of the room, slamming the door behind her. "Don't you notice how she barely eats? And she goes to the bathroom all the time?"

I didn't tell them about the time I'd caught her in the bathroom at the yogurt place. Even though I was almost positive she'd been lying about not feeling well, I figured there was no point in revealing that part.

"That's a big accusation," Noelle said.

"It's a big deal," I said. "I know. That's why

it's been so hard to carry this secret inside me."

"It's not even really a secret, is it?" Christina asked. "It's more like speculation. You just didn't want to have to spill one of your own secrets."

I don't know what reaction I'd been expecting. Maybe that was the problem—I hadn't stopped to think about the various ways this could have blown up in my face. But still, I felt tears sting my eyes, and I tried to blink them away before the other girls noticed.

"I said I *think*. I *think* she has an eating disorder. You guys don't see that something is up? Seriously? I could tell she was acting weird from the second I got here, and I've only been training with you guys for a few weeks. You've trained with her for years. You didn't see anything wrong?"

"There's a difference between dieting and a disorder," Noelle said. "I know you came from a smaller gym, Britt, but at the Elite level it's very common to watch your weight. You have to. It's just part of the training."

Maybe I'd gone to a less competitive gym before, but I'd seen behavior like Jessie's. At Loveland, Kim had started using those disgusting laxatives when the regionals were coming up, because she thought they would help her. Instead, they had ended up making her so weak she'd had to withdraw from the meet.

"Don't you get it?" My voice was becoming squeaky; I tried to calm myself down. "That's why she can get away with it. That's why nobody does anything. She says she wants to lose weight for the qualifier, and everyone gives her a pat on the back. Nobody stops to think about how she's doing it!"

Christina's eyes were jet black, and I could tell I'd lost any ground I might have gained with her during that one hour when we all played Rock Band together like friends, or at least like a team. I had more than lost it—I had gone miles in the other direction. "I forgot to add the other reason why I don't like you," she said. "You get into everybody's business. You're here for two seconds and you start giving me advice on my gymnastics, going through Noelle's stuff, and spreading nasty rumors about Jessie. *It's not all about you.*"

I tried to blink back the tears that I felt gathering. Her words stung, because I'd heard them just hours before—from Dionne, when she'd called me out for monopolizing her party. Maybe I would have been a lot better off if I'd kept my head down and worried only about my gymnastics. But in this case, I *knew* I was right. Why did nobody else see it?

"I'm going to check on Jessie," Noelle said. She hesitated, then gave me an apologetic look. "It might be best if you aren't here when she comes back, Britt."

"You want me to go home?" Tears were streaming down my face now, and I hiccupped on the last word. "I can't call my mother and tell her to come get me. She'd want to know why, and I don't—"

I don't want to admit to her that I'm universally hated at the fancy new gym where I'm training. I don't want her to know that her daughter is a pariah.

"Just sleep in the den," Christina said. "I'll tell my mom you weren't feeling well."

It wasn't so far from the truth, at that point. I felt like I could've thrown up. Silently, I dragged my duffel bag out of Christina's room. I hadn't ended up needing the bathing suit, the change of clothes, or the air freshener. The only thing that stank around here was me.

Jessie was sitting on the couch when I arrived in the family room, and for several moments we just stared at each other.

"Look," I said, "I'm sorry—"

"You promised."

I could tell she'd been crying, but her voice wasn't quavering now.

"I know, but I'm worried about you. I only want to help you, Jessie. Please believe me."

Noelle appeared in the doorway and looked nervously from Jessie's face to mine. "I was looking for you," she said to Jessie. "Come on, we're going to watch a movie in Christina's room."

As she passed me, Jessie deliberately turned so our shoulders didn't touch. When she was just beyond me, she paused. "It wasn't your secret to tell," she said in a low voice.

How could I explain to her that it had been starting to feel like my secret? That I lay in bed at night worrying that my only friend in Texas was destroying herself, and I had no idea how to stop it?

"It wasn't your secret," she said again, so quietly that I doubted Noelle could hear her. And then she and Noelle were gone, leaving me alone in the family room. I sat on the uncomfortable leather couch listening to the ceiling fan whoosh in the otherwise quiet house and cried.

* * *

I didn't sleep well that night, but somehow I dozed off around three in the morning, and when I woke up, my head throbbed and my mouth felt like cotton. From the kitchen, I could hear laughter and the sound of plates clacking against the table and pans being moved around the stove. Judging by the smell, Mrs. Flores was making eggs. The glowing numbers on the cable box said that it was already eleven o'clock.

I was still wearing my shirt and capris from the night before, and I knew my hair was all matted on one side, but I didn't bother about my appearance as I headed into the kitchen. What did I care? If they were going to hate me, let them. I was done trying to impress them.

As expected, the girls grew silent when I stepped into the room, as though my presence formed a vacuum, sucking a room dry of any happy noise. Then Christina started giggling, as though she had been reminded of some hilarious joke at my expense.

Whatever. I sat down at the table and ignored them. "Are there any more eggs?" I asked.

"Britt, I'm sorry," Mrs. Flores said. "Christina said you weren't feeling well, so we didn't save you any."

I glanced around the kitchen and saw that all the dishes had been put in the sink. Everyone was obviously done eating.

"Would you like some cereal?" Mrs. Flores asked. "I think we have some oat crunch."

That stuff tasted like squirrel food, but I nodded as though it were my favorite meal in the whole world. Mrs. Flores poured me a bowl. I'd taken only one bite when the doorbell rang.

"Oh, Mrs. Morgan!" I heard Mrs. Flores say. The sound of my chewing seemed deafening.

"Please, call me Pamela," my mom said; she seemed breathless. I was trying to figure out why she sounded so . . . happy. And then I remembered. The painting.

Crap. There was no way that the other girls were going to agree to help out now.

"Hi, honey," my mom said, entering the kitchen and stopping to press a kiss on my forehead. "Good thing you wore an old shirt you can paint in. Girls, do you want to change before we head over?"

The shirt was *not* old. I loved that shirt. Why did everyone seem to think that it was something off *What Not to Wear*? Okay, so most of the sparkles had fallen off, and the hem was a little stretched out.

"Head over where?" Noelle asked.

My mom glanced at me, then at Mrs. Flores. "Didn't Brittany mention the painting party?"

I closed my eyes.

"I'm opening my own day care," my mom explained. "And I need to paint the classrooms today. I was hoping to recruit the girls with the promise of some pizza. . . . I thought Britt had already asked everyone."

"We can't have pizza," Christina said. "It'll interfere with our training."

"It's very common for gymnasts to watch what they eat," Jessie added, giving me a pointed look.

My mom nodded enthusiastically, as though pleased that the choice of food was the only impediment to her plan. "That's right, I remember Britt mentioning that. . . . Well, we could get something else instead. Mrs. Flores, would it be all right with you if I borrowed the girls for a couple of hours?"

"Oh . . ." Mrs. Flores seemed to feel put on the spot, but eventually she gave a wide, fake smile. "Sure, I don't see why not. Jessie, your mom wasn't going to pick you up until three, and Noelle was going to stay over here to do homework with Christina anyway."

Three pairs of eyes were glaring at me, but I just took a spoonful of my cereal so large that milk oozed out of the corners of my mouth. Why should I let a little bit of old-fashioned hatred ruin my appetite?

If my mom noticed that everyone at the day care was more strained than smiling, she didn't mention it. She was her usual too-chipper self, handing out brushes and painter's tape.

"I chose bright colors because I wanted the rooms to look cheerful," she said. "Don't you think that's important for kids? To have happy colors?"

"Super important," I mumbled.

She sighed with satisfaction. "This is going to be a whole new era, Britt. Just you wait and see."

She gave me one of the smaller brushes to do the edges with. It was like she didn't know me at all. There were some people who had very fine hand-eye coordination. I was not one of them. I could flip backward and manage to catch the beam with my hands, but ask me to play a game of Operation and I was zapping myself all over the place trying to get the stupid organ pieces out of the guy's body.

I made up for it by painting very slowly. At least, that's what I told myself. But I also took my time because I didn't really feel like doing it, and I figured that this way I could paint as little as possible.

Christina and Jessie were on the other side of the room, using rollers to cover the entire wall with yellow paint. They were laughing and trying to paint over each other's strokes as though they were competing for territory. I wished that I could've had that job.

Noelle also had a little brush, but she had soon done twice the area I had covered in the same time. When I actually looked at it, there were no drips or smears, either. Was there *anything* she wasn't good at?

Even my mother noticed. "Nice job, Noelle," she said, coming to stand behind her. "You're a natural. Have you painted before?"

Noelle stepped back to survey her work. "I helped my parents paint their store," she said. "I like to paint. It's relaxing."

"Well, you're a hard worker! Any time you'd like to help out around the day care, I'm sure I could find something for you." My mom crossed over to where I was standing on a stepladder, slathering paint onto the corner by a doorway.

"Britt, you have to be more careful!" She took

the brush from my hand and turned it so that the bristles were angled correctly for the tight space. "You see how I'm making it as small as possible, so I can get a neat line of paint in there? If you do it your way, we'll have to repaint the entire door!"

She handed me back the brush, but not before making a clucking sound and bending down to wipe away a drop of paint on the doorjamb. She licked her thumb and rubbed at it, but a very light tint of color still remained.

As she headed back into the other classroom, which she was painting a vibrant orange, she touched Noelle's shoulder. "Keep up the good work," she said.

I know that my mother probably justified having Elite gymnasts paint her day care by pretending that this was somehow a team-building exercise. I watched Noelle charm my mother while Jessie and Christina laughed over in the corner, and I guessed that the whole experience might be bringing them closer together.

Me, I'd never felt less part of anything in my life.

Twelve

At practice on Monday, I tried really hard to pretend I didn't care when Christina shot me dirty looks, or when Noelle ignored me, or when Jessie's eyes accused me of breaking my promise. I did my half routines, focusing on making each one perfect so I could move on to the next set. Out of the corner of my eye, I could see Jessie and Christina over with Cheng, working on their vaults. Jessie was opening up too early, and she looked tired. But of course, I had no right to tell her those things anymore. We weren't friends.

When I finally talked to Noelle, I kept my voice

light, just so she wouldn't think I was like a dog with its tail between its legs or something. "I bet you I can land my full twist on the beam three times in a row," I said.

Noelle glanced nervously toward the front of the gym. Mo had disappeared into the office for a second to take a phone call. "We're not supposed to be practicing our acrobatic series without supervision," Noelle said. "We're just doing the leaps and dance elements right now."

"How much do you want to bet?"

"How much do I want to bet that you'll get into *huge* trouble?" Noelle said. "Nothing, because I already know the outcome. You *will* get into huge trouble, and I don't want to be dragged into it with you."

"I'll bet you Sparky," I said, my gaze flicking over her gym bag, where I knew the stuffed dog was safely stored. I was goading her on purpose, and I didn't care. If Boo Radley had known that all the neighborhood kids were making fun of him, he probably would've gotten them right back. Even a freak who locks himself in his house knows that sometimes the best defense is a good offense.

Noelle turned white. "Don't be ridiculous."

"Keep count," I said, and set myself up for the first in the series. I crouched down before throwing my arms back for momentum, propelling myself backward, my body already twisting. When my feet hit the beam, they were totally flat, my toes curling around the edges of the apparatus to maintain my balance.

I took a deep breath. "One."

Noelle didn't even pretend she was still working on her pirouette. "Britt, *please*," she said, glancing toward the office.

"Your wish is my command," I said, and executed a second flawless standing full twist. I was on fire! I almost wished Mo could see this. She'd have let me put it back in my routine for sure.

"You've made your point," Noelle hissed. "Can we get back to work now? Please?"

"This *is* work," I said. "This is me working on the skill that's going to make me national champion one day." I saw Mo emerge from the office, but a woman stopped her to chat. "Watch this. Third time's a charm."

I knew from the moment my feet left the beam that I didn't have the height. My timing had been a little off, my movements too jerky, and I hadn't been able to fling my body backward with as much momentum as I usually did. It seemed like I was suspended in the air forever.

My head hit the beam squarely, and I scraped my cheek as I slid down the side of it and crumpled to the floor.

"Britt!" Noelle jumped down from her beam and knelt beside me. "Britt, say something!"

But I couldn't speak. I had the words in my head: *I'm okay*, or even, *What goes up must come down, right?* But they wouldn't come out of my mouth.

And then I saw Mo's face looming over me. She told Noelle to move aside. Her hands were light as they skimmed over my body, my shoulders, my neck, asking me what hurt and what I could move. Once she was certain I didn't have a broken neck or back, she helped me to my feet. She walked with me, supporting my weight so gently I barely registered that we had already crossed the whole gym and were in her office.

Then she sat me down, and her eyes were not gentle.

"Very dangerous, what you did," she said.

"I'm okay," I said. I really did feel fine. I must've

been a little dazed earlier, but other than a slight headache, I was ready to go back out there and continue practice. But when I suggested that to Mo, she shook her head.

"You go home," she said. "No more practice for you."

"For today? Or ever?" I asked the question, but I didn't actually fear the answer. Of course it would just be for today. I'd taken a little fall, but that was it. There was no reason for it to derail my whole future in this sport.

But Mo's face told a different story. "I have to think about," she said. "You took risk."

"I thought that's what made me a good gymnast," I said. "I take risks. I did a full twist at the competition where you saw my tape, and I did two standing back fulls in a row today. Perfectly! You should have seen them."

"Two standing back fulls mean nothing if you paralyzed," Mo said.

"I'm not." I waved my arms and held up my foot, rotating the ankle. "See? I was just a little shocked before. But I'm fine."

Mo steepled her fingers and paused, as though she had something difficult to say and was trying to think of the best way to put it. That was when I started to get really scared.

"You don't listen," she said finally. "You don't follow rule. A gymnast is worthless to me if she don't listen."

I started to protest, but Mo picked up the phone. "I call your mother," she said. "She come get you."

The car ride home was silent; when I tried to talk to my mother, she said that she had a lot to think about. As soon as we got home, she said she was going to her room to do some of that thinking and suggested I do the same.

I wanted to call Dionne, but we hadn't talked since the time I had hung up on her. She'd actually called me, but I'd told my mother to tell her I was out. It wasn't that I didn't want to talk to Dionne. Once I had gotten over my initial shock that she was apparently still mad at me for something that had happened almost a year ago, I had felt bad. I *had* kind of monopolized her party, and I knew that sometimes I could be a little self-centered. I realized that all those times I'd turned things into the Britt Show, as she called it, I'd made people want to stop tuning in, and that was one of the reasons I felt so alone now. I wanted to apologize to her. I wanted my friend back.

But with everything that was going on with Jessie and at the gym, I hadn't felt as if I could handle anything else. Now I missed her, but I worried that every day that passed without us talking made it that much harder for us to make up.

When my mom finally called me down to dinner, I was surprised to see my dad there, too. He usually worked until late at night, which meant he came home after I was in bed and slept most of the day while I was being homeschooled by Grandma. It was rare to see him at dinner, since that was the meal he was always cooking for other people.

"Hi, Dad," I said, trying to act like I didn't already know the reason he was home. He kissed my cheek but looked at me as though he had a big presentation later that night and people were going to expect him to report on everything he had observed about me.

Dinner was homemade macaroni and cheese, the kind with six different cheeses, which my dad could whip up in no time. Although I'd never have told him this, a part of me preferred the processed version made with orange powder. His macaroni and cheese had won awards and everything, but I guess I was just used to having the instant version, from all the nights we'd made dinner without him. There's something comforting about the way the orange sauce congeals on top of the macaroni.

I'd finished most of the food on my plate when my father finally turned to me. "Do you know why we made the move to Texas?"

"Gary—"

He held up his hand. "Pam, she needs to hear this. Do you know why?"

I wanted to say, *Because it's warmer?* But I sensed that this was not the time for jokes. "No."

"We moved here so that you could go to Texas Twisters. We didn't come here and then find the gym. We came here *because* of the gym. Do you know what that means?"

My grandmother had taught me about rhetorical questions last year. She'd said they were questions that you weren't supposed to respond to. I'd asked her what the point was of a question with no answer, and she'd said that it often meant that both parties knew what the answer should be. According to her, if you actually tried to answer the question, it would just seem rude. Apparently you're supposed to let the person just ramble on and make the point both of you know he's trying to make, without interruption.

I didn't think this question was rhetorical, though, because I still didn't completely know what it meant that my parents had moved here for my gym. The full implications of it were just starting to sink in. Still, I didn't say anything.

"That means that we drove for two days for you. We sold our house in Ohio, left our friends, left our jobs . . . all for you."

"Gary," my mom said quietly, "don't make her feel guilty."

"She should feel a little guilty," he said. "She should feel guilty that we've made sacrifices and she's throwing it all away because she can't stop goofing off. Do you like gymnastics?"

It took me a minute to realize he'd shifted from talking about me to talking to me. I wasn't sure how he wanted me to respond, so I just stared at him. I wished my grandmother were there, but there was an exhibit at the museum she'd wanted to see. She'd probably made herself scarce on purpose, because she was smart like that.

"Do you?" he repeated. "Answer the question."

"Sorry," I said. "I thought it was rhetorical."

My mom tried to suppress a smile, but my dad wasn't having it. "It's not rhetorical," he said. "It's an actual question, and one which you shouldn't have to think about too hard. Do you like gymnastics?"

It was true—I didn't have to think about it too hard. Even though I hated the tedium of drills sometimes, even though I hated all the stretches they made you do, even though I complained about beam and resisted ballet training to improve my floor work, I really loved every second of it. It was the one place where I felt truly free.

"Yes," I said.

"Do you want to be a champion?"

"Yes. More than anything else in the whole world."

His face softened, and he looked more like the dad I remembered: the scruffy face, crinkly smile, and twinkling blue eyes of someone I could joke with and tell things to. I realized I'd missed him since we'd moved to Texas.

"We don't want to force you into anything," he said. "You know that, right, monkey? But we want you to have the opportunity to achieve your dream, and we thought this would be the best place for that. I'd just hate to see you throw it away."

"I won't," I whispered.

Maybe I hadn't kept my promise to Jessie. Maybe it wasn't one I was meant to keep. But this was a promise I would see through.

All of this had to be worth it, right? Moving to a new city; leaving the safety and comfort of Loveland behind; saying good-bye to Dionne, my best friend since I was eight; alienating the only three girls I'd met so far, who happened to also be my teammates; failing to prove myself to my coach, who obviously thought I was reckless and immature.

My grandmother wanted me to put myself in other people's shoes, the way Atticus told Scout to do in *To Kill a Mockingbird*. But sometimes it was hard enough to wear my own shoes, when I couldn't tell if they were getting me anywhere.

Thirteen

First thing next morning, I marched
into Mo's office.

"I'm sorry about yesterday," I said. "It won't happen again. I'm listening. Please just tell me what to do."

She looked at me as if weighing my words. "Get out there and run laps around the floor until girls get here. Then you can stretch with them."

I'd be lying if I said I didn't balk a little bit in my mind at that. I'd dragged myself out of bed thirty minutes earlier than usual to get to practice before anybody else and talk to Mo, and the idea of running circles around the blue mat sounded like the

163

biggest waste of time. But I didn't say any of that to Mo, as I might have just the day before. Instead, I nodded and headed out to the floor.

I don't know if it was something about the monotonous pounding of my feet or the constant left turns, but as I jogged I started to think. I thought about what my dad had said the night before, about my whole family uprooting itself so that I could train at one of the best gyms in the country. I thought about my mother's opening the day care, and how excited she'd been to change the colors of a couple of rooms to put her personal touch on them. Mostly, I thought about Jessie.

It was possible that I was being a drama queen. Maybe everyone else was right. Jessie had one of the biggest meets of her life coming up, and of course she'd be looking for anything that might help her performance. It was true that gymnasts at the highest levels had to watch what they ate and keep to a strict diet in order to ensure that their bodies were in peak condition. Wasn't that what being an athlete was about?

But then I remembered again the way her knees had looked, red and scraped from kneeling on that bathroom floor in the yogurt place. She hadn't been sick that day; I felt it in my gut. I remembered the way she admired other gymnasts' thinness on television and made comments about gymnasts who she thought could stand to lose a few pounds. I remembered all the times I'd seen her during snack break, or at the frozen yogurt place, or at her house, or at Christina's house, not eating, not eating . . . always not eating. Maybe it was just a diet. But it had gone too far.

The question was what to do about it. Obviously, bringing it up during a game of Truth or Dare had not been the brightest idea. I had to talk to someone who would actually listen, someone who could help Jessie. But who?

I saw Mo in the office, her head bent over something at her desk. Before I could have second thoughts, I ran over to her door. I stood there, panting, as she looked up.

"If this how you listen—" she said, but I cut her off.

"I know I'm supposed to be doing laps," I said. "And I will. I'll do as many laps as you want me to. I'm even ready to start those ballet classes you mentioned. But I have something I need to talk about with you first. Is that okay?"

She inclined her head, and I pulled up a chair. "It's about Jessie. . . ."

And then I told her everything. I told her about Jessie never eating during snack time, Jessie throwing up at the yogurt place, Jessie commenting on how thin the gymnasts at the American Invitational were. I tried to stick to just the facts, not coloring them with my perceptions. Mo had dealt with gymnasts for longer than I'd been alive. If she didn't think that Jessie's behavior sounded problematic, then obviously I *was* in the wrong. I just didn't think so.

Mo let me talk without interrupting, and when I was done, she asked only one thing. "Have you talked to Jessie?"

I nodded. "And the other—" I almost mentioned that the other girls didn't seem to think she had a problem, either. But I didn't want them to find out and think I'd thrown them under the bus. This was about Jessie. "I just have a really strong feeling about this."

Mo put her hand on my shoulder. "You have good instinct," she said. "You need to listen to it more."

I snorted. I couldn't help myself. Wasn't that

my problem? That I went with my gut instead of listening to authority? It seemed like that was what had gotten me into a lot of these messes in the first place.

"Yeah, right," I said to Mo. "Like my instinct to show off on the beam, until I fell and could've hurt myself. Or my instinct to show off in front of Christina, until I made her hate me."

Mo smiled. "Perhaps you see pattern not to show off," she said. "Sometime it not about power. Yes?"

I still believed that a full twist on the balance beam was the biggest, coolest move I could do, but I understood that Mo was talking about more than gymnastics. Even in competitions, you couldn't just do trick after trick if you wanted a high score. You had to use those little connecting moves to help tell a story to the judges. Those little moves could seem pointless, but without them, your whole routine would fall apart.

Mo's eyes turned thoughtful. "Deep down, you know what to do. But then you second-guess yourself and get in trouble. If you follow what's in here"—she gestured toward my heart—"you be just fine."

It was the most obvious advice in the world. It had probably been written on a thousand Hallmark cards. And yet this time it felt like an epiphany, like something was changing inside me that I couldn't change back—as if I'd ever want to.

In the middle of practice, Mo called Jessie into the office. Jessie came out a little later, crying. Mo hadn't thought it would be a good idea for me to sit in on the meeting, and I was kind of relieved. But of course, Jessie knew who had talked to Mo.

I followed Jessie into the locker room. "Just listen to me," I said. "Please."

She turned around, not bothering to hide her red-rimmed eyes and quivering chin. "Haven't you done enough talking? God, as if it's not bad enough that you told Christina and Noelle. At least they weren't stupid enough to believe you. But then you have to go and tell Mo? That's really low, Britt."

"I knew you'd be mad at me," I said. "I knew you'd probably hate me forever. But I'd rather you hate me forever than do this to yourself. Did I ever tell you about Kim, back at my old gym?"

Jessie chewed her left thumbnail, her *no*

so quiet and sullen that I almost thought I'd imagined it.

"Well, she had a problem, and you really remind me of her. One time, my friend Dionne and I caught her in the bathroom with these laxatives she was using to lose weight, and—"

"I've never used laxatives in my life," Jessie said. "That's disgusting."

"Maybe not, but you and I both know that you're obsessed with your weight, just like Kim was. I don't think you see yourself in the mirror anymore."

"I'm ugly," she cried. "Why would I want to see myself?"

"You're not ugly. That image you're making up is ugly. I don't want to be friends with that girl."

"Well, she doesn't want to be friends with you!"

I shrugged. "I can't help that. But I can help you, or at least try."

"Some help," Jessie snorted. "Thanks to you, I'm probably not going to the qualifier, not after Mo meets with my parents. Can you believe that? I'm going to have to wait even longer to become an Elite. Christina will make it, and I'll be the last person still training as a stupid Level Ten."

"Maybe it's for the best," I said, but it sounded

weak even to my ears. I hadn't known that Jessie would be left out of the qualifier. If the pressure to compete was part of her stress, then it made sense that Jessie's parents and Mo might want her to take it easy and help her focus on getting better. But I was getting better at imagining myself in someone else's shoes, and I knew I'd have been devastated if I lost the chance to move up to Elite-level competition.

The chances that I'd completely wrecked my friendship with Jessie were high. But at the same time, I couldn't regret what I'd done. I might have been the least-liked member of the Texas Twisters team, but I was beginning to realize that teamwork wasn't always just about getting along. It was about looking out for one another, even if it meant making hard decisions. And this had been the hardest decision I'd ever made in my life.

It was easy to keep my head down and just concentrate on gymnastics during practice. Jessie had been sent home, and the other girls wouldn't even meet my gaze. After I did five perfect first halves of my beam routine, Mo stopped me. "I think we add full twist," she said.

I knew better than to get my hopes up, but I still felt my adrenaline surge. "Really? A standing back full?"

She flicked her wrist dismissively. "You not ready for that. But you could do a round-off to full twist for your acrobatic series. I think you can handle."

I would've jumped up and down, but that wasn't the best idea when standing on a surface that was only four inches wide. Obviously, Mo could see that I was really ready to change. Otherwise, why would she have finally decided to trust me?

Apparently, Mo was wary of letting me get too excited. "For now, you do only on practice beam. Is that clear?"

"Yes," I said. Kind of a bummer, but still way better than not being able to try the move at all. The practice beam was shorter and had mats stacked up on either side so you never fell too far. When I was younger, I used to love the practice beam, because it meant I was doing something cooler than anything they'd allow me to do on a regular beam. But now, it felt a little bit like being told you have to sit in a flight simulator when you've already orbited the moon.

Still, I wasn't going to complain. The New Britt would never complain.

I was smiling as I started working on the second half of my beam routine. Noelle gave me a weird look. She was probably wondering what I could possibly have been happy about, given everything that was going on.

It did give me a pang when I glanced over at the other side of the gym and saw Christina and Cheng at the bars. Jessie should have been there, working on her transitions from low bar to high bar and trying to stick her dismount. But she wasn't, and it was all my fault.

"Why would you do it?" Noelle asked, her voice low. She was still standing on her beam, hands on her hips, looking at me. Mo had been pulled aside by a parent; I glanced over to see if there was any chance she might catch us talking. She moved slightly to her right, and I saw that the parent was Jessie's mom.

I wanted to tell Noelle that I'd had to, but when I opened my mouth, no words came out. Had I really? What if I'd waited until after the qualifier, at least, so Jessie could've had her chance to compete? Should I have thought it through?

"You don't know any of us," Noelle said. "You think you do, but you've only been here a few weeks."

It was weird how it felt like so much longer. I tried to remember messing around in the pit with Dionne, pretending that we were competing in the X Games as we spun like cyclones into the soft foam. Had I really been doing that only a few months ago? It was hard even to picture that Britt now—the one who just had fun without worrying about the consequences, the one who hadn't known what it was like to compete for a team. There had been Dionne, and there had been me, and we had been friends without really worrying about how we might get in each other's way in the gym. Maybe that was the way to do it.

"If you think this will get to Christina and stop her from qualifying, you're wrong," Noelle said.

Honestly, it hadn't even occurred to me to worry about Christina. This wasn't about my beef with her; I didn't really even *have* a beef. Christina was the one who seemed to have it in for *me*. This had nothing to do with Christina, and I told Noelle that.

"What about Jessie?" I asked. I hated the idea

173

that anything I'd done would damage Jessie, and I needed reassurance that she'd be okay. I knew Christina was tough, but Jessie was different.

Noelle looked down at the beam, smoothing a line of chalk with her toe. "Just give her time," she said. "She'll be okay."

Did Noelle mean that Jessie would return to her training without any problems? Was Noelle acknowledging the fact that Jessie *wasn't* okay now, that she did have some issues? Or did she mean that Jessie would eventually forgive me?

From my vantage point up on the beam, I watched Mo and Jessie's mother talk, and I tried to figure out what was happening. Mo's back was to me, but I could see Jessie's mom's face, the way her forehead was all crinkled up so that her freckles looked like little raisins. She was nodding at whatever Mo was saying, pressing her hand to her chest as though taking responsibility for something.

Noelle went back to her drills, and I watched her execute an absolutely perfect full turn with her leg held up the whole time. She looked like one of those ballerinas in a music box, spinning on the toes of one foot without even a wobble.

Maybe it wouldn't hurt to take those extra

ballet lessons that Mo kept telling my mother I should have. I knew that both Christina and Noelle did them once a week, and they were two of the best dancers I'd ever seen. Especially Christina, who—as much as I hated to admit it—looked like she could have starred in *Swan Lake* if she'd wanted to. Well, if *Swan Lake* had also included some back walkovers and ring leaps, which, although I'd never actually seen it, I kind of doubted. My mom took me to see *The Nutcracker* one year for Christmas, and I'd sat through most of the show trying to figure out how the nutcracker guy got into that crazy costume. If all they were going to do was twirl around the stage a bunch, what was the point? Why not throw in some backflips?

We did our stretches at the end of practice as usual, and my mom was actually on time to pick me up. After the long day I'd had and the added stress of the whole Jessie situation, I was relieved to see her red car pull up near the parking lot.

"Hi," I said, climbing into the passenger side. I sighed as soon as my head hit the seat.

My mom gave me a sideways glance. "Did your chat with Mo go well?" she asked.

How to explain to my mom the completely

complicated situation our talk had created? For the moment, I chose to forget about the whole Jessie part and just tell my mom what I knew she was waiting to hear. "Yeah. Mo even said I could put the full twist back into my beam routine."

"That's great, honey!"

I felt myself get excited all over again. "It was totally cool. I mean, I'll be on the practice beam for a little while, but that's not so bad. As long as I get to rock it in competition. Can you imagine me on TV someday, Mom? Landing a full twist on two feet perfectly, without bobbling or anything?"

"Mm-hmm," she murmured, but I could tell she was distracted by having to merge lanes; she put on her turn signal and started glancing over her shoulder.

"I know I won't be on TV for a while," I said. "But someday, when I'm a Senior Elite, I bet I could be. Imagine if I went to the American Invitational. Or the Olympics!"

"Noelle—she's the state beam champ, right?" my mom asked, obviously just putting Noelle's name together with the gigantic sign that hung on the out-side of the gym. I could still remember the first time I'd ever seen Texas Twisters, driving by it at night in our U-Haul and peering through the windows.

"Yeah. She's really good."

"She's such a hard worker," my mom said. "And seems like a sweet girl. You should ask her for any help you need with your beam routine. I bet you could learn a lot from her."

I doubted anyone would ever have thought to call me a hard worker. Grandma used to give me assignments that she said she wasn't going to look at but that were for my own "personal edification," whatever that meant. Then she realized that as soon as she said that, I would just doodle all over my paper, or sometimes write the same nonsense sentence over and over to make it look as if I was writing. It wasn't that I didn't know how to do the work—I just didn't really want to. Grandma said if I spent half as much energy actually doing what people asked of me as I did trying to get *out* of doing what people asked of me, I'd have been a force to be reckoned with.

But that was the Old Britt. The New Britt would run a hundred laps around the gym if that was what Mo wanted, or write twenty pages on the themes of *To Kill a Mockingbird*. The New Britt could be just as hard a worker as Noelle was.

Still, I doubted that anyone would ever have called me sweet. I wasn't bitter or anything, but I wasn't the kind of person who would break off half of my candy bar to give to a starving orphan, either.

But that was also the Old Britt. The New Britt was going to be pleasant to everyone, even Christina and Noelle, who didn't seem to want to return the favor. I hoped my mom could see how hard I was trying.

Fourteen

As soon as we got home, my mom disappeared into her bedroom like she usually did. I stood in the living room for a second before knocking on her door. Although I didn't hear her tell me to, I went in anyway.

She already had the TV tuned to some show about supernannies, where these women with British accents were always telling parents it was "all about boundaries." I reached over and switched the TV off.

"Britt! I was watching that."

"Could I talk to you for a minute?" I asked. "It's really important."

Maybe it was because I was feeling energized, as the New Britt, maybe it was because I'd already braved two huge confrontations that day, with Mo and with Jessie, although those hadn't been very successful. But all I knew was that I didn't want things to be the same as before.

"I'm sorry that you and Dad had to move all the way here for me," I said. "I know you liked it in Ohio."

"Oh, honey." My mom patted a spot next to her on the bed, and I plopped down to join her. "He shouldn't have said that."

"I'm glad he did," I said. "I had no idea how much I was messing everything up."

"You need to know that we take your gymnastics seriously. So you should, too."

"I know." It was the next part that was the hardest for me to say. The part that, no matter how many times I rehearsed it in my head, I didn't know quite how to phrase; finally I figured I would just ask it straight out and not care how stupid it sounded. "You love me, right, Mom?"

She laughed. "What kind of a question is that? Of course I love you."

"You don't wish that I was smarter, or better,

or . . . more like Noelle?" From what I knew of Noelle's parents, who were Romanian immigrants, it didn't seem like they had a single bit of trouble from Noelle. She would never put glue in the water fountain (it was *supposed* to be a fun prank, but Dionne and I had to clean the glue out, and then it wasn't so fun) or talk back to her grandmother about the absolute uselessness of converting decimals to fractions using arithmetic (that's what a calculator is for, after all).

"Of course not." Her brows drew together as she studied my face. "Why are you asking all of these questions? Where is this coming from?"

"It's just that you spend a lot of time at the day care." The words came out in a rush, as though I was worried they'd get stale if they stayed inside me too long. "Sometimes I think other people's kids get to see you more than I do. And that sucks, because I don't have another mother to go home to like they do. I have you, but you're always busy. And then you say that Noelle is so great, and it seems like maybe you'd spend more time with me if I was like her."

"Oh, Brittany." She pulled me close to her, stroking my cheek and burying her face in my hair.

"I didn't know you felt that way. I know I haven't been around a lot lately—"

"Well, you're starting your own day care," I said. "It's your dream, I know, like I spend all my time at gym, because my dream is to go to the Olympics. I guess I just miss you. And Dad."

"We both love you very much. You. Not Noelle or the kids at the day care, but my spunky, smart little Britt. Don't forget that. And we'll figure out a way to spend more time together, I promise."

Twelve's a little old for this kind of warm and fuzzy sitcom moment, probably, but it felt good to curl up on the bed with my mom and find an old movie on TV. After all, a lot had changed since I'd moved to the second-biggest state in the country. I'd left behind a friend who got my sense of humor and understood that, while I could be thoughtless sometimes, I was never malicious. I'd given up a spot at a gym where, even if they didn't produce Olympic champions, they knew that having fun was just as important as winning medals.

I couldn't stand the thought that I might've hurt my parents, too, so it was good to know that they were on my side. The New Britt might have been more mature than the Old Britt, but one thing hadn't changed—at the end of the day, I still needed my mom.

After dinner, I picked up the phone and dialed Dionne's number. Her mom answered.

"Um, hi," I said, suddenly nervous. I hadn't expected Dionne's mother to pick up her cell phone. What if Dionne had told her what a bad friend I was? What if she'd already told her to screen any call from me with some lame excuse about being in the shower or out with friends?

Or what if she really *was* out? Dionne had had other friends besides me, and they'd probably gotten superclose after I left. Dionne might even have been wondering why she'd wasted so much time with me when she could have been hanging out with them all along.

Meanwhile, I had no friends here. Worse, I had mortal enemies.

"Is Dionne home?"

"Sure, just one second." Dionne must have deleted me from her contacts. Obviously, her mother didn't recognize my voice, or else she wouldn't have been so cavalier about handing her daughter the phone.

"Hello?"

"Hi, Dionne. It's me, Britt."

"I know." So obviously she hadn't deleted me from her address book. Maybe she wasn't mad at me after all. "What's up?"

"Not much," I said. "Is this still your number? Or is it your mom's now?"

"It's mine. The phone was just on the counter, so she picked it up. I hate it when she does that."

"At least you have a cell phone." It was a familiar discussion, and I felt myself relax a little bit. "I'd rather have a cell phone with a thousand restrictions than no cell phone at all."

"True. So what's up? I called you a couple times."

Where did I even begin? I explained to Dionne the whole situation with Jessie, the way the other girls treated me, the truth about why my parents moved here, and the conversation I'd had with my mom.

"Wow," she said when I was done. "You've been busy. I was going to tell you about how I invented a new cereal by combining Rice Krispies with Cocoa Puffs, but now it doesn't seem so important."

"You were right," I blurted out. "I should've

stopped to think about your feelings at your birthday party. I'm sorry."

"Don't worry about it," she said. "You wouldn't be Britt without being totally crazy."

"Great. Just what I want to be known for."

Dionne laughed. "You're not," she said. "Well, okay, sometimes. But you dive right into something headfirst and worry about the consequences later, and that can be a really cool way to be."

"Yeah," I said. "If you don't end up with brain damage."

We chatted for an hour. I laughed at all of her stories about people at our old gym, and she tried to figure out a time when she could come down to visit. We were cool, just like we'd always been. It felt good to have a friend.

This time, it was my mother who told us to get off the phone. "I gotta go," I said. "I'm about to play Battleship with my mom, and I've got a strategy that's going to help me win big, I just know it."

"Is it your thing where you put all your ships on one side of the board? Everyone sees right through that."

Crap. That had been exactly my plan.

* * *

I didn't have a strategy for talking to Jessie after the incident the week before, except that I knew I had to do it. I told my mom that I thought I'd left something over at Jessie's, so she stopped by the sprawling suburban house on our way from the gym to the grocery store.

"You'll be only a second, though, right?" she said, glancing at her watch. "You know the frozen lasagna will take two hours to cook once we get it in the oven."

"I'll be quick," I assured her. It was probably not a lie. Worst-case scenario: Jessie would see me through the peephole and unleash her hounds (she didn't have dogs before, but she would have them now, to protect herself against me), and it only took them a few moments to tear me to shreds. Of course, best-case scenario was that Jessie and I would totally make up, and then I would run back and tell my mom to count me out for dinner, because I was going to spend the night with my new best friend.

Like that would happen.

Tiffany opened the door when I rang the bell. She stared at me as if I'd come from an entirely different planet. I was still in my leotard, with my shorts pulled over it, while she was wearing a baby T and low-rise jeans and looked as if she should have been on the cover of a teen magazine, so I guess I might as well have been an alien.

"Hi!" I smiled to let her know that I came in peace. "I'm, uh, one of Jessie's friends. Is she here?"

Tiffany's eyes flicked over me again. "Come in," she said grudgingly. "Jess is in her room."

She led me through the kitchen toward the closed door of Jessie's room. I smiled again at her, trying to tell her with my eyes that everything was cool and she could leave me alone now, but she just stood there.

"Go ahead," she said. "Knock. She's in there."

My hands were trembling a little, but I wanted to look confident, so I ended up rapping on the door way harder than I meant to. It sounded as if I was the police coming to break up a party or something. "Jess?"

There was silence for a moment. Then, through the door: "Who is it?"

At that point, I could have told her Adolf Hitler and she'd probably have been more likely to open the door. "Um, it's Britt. From gym."

I don't know why I felt the need to add that

last part. I'm sure she knew exactly who I was.

The response was swift. "Go away!"

Tiffany raised her eyebrows. "I don't think she wants to see you," she said.

Thank you, Captain Obvious.

"Jess, please," I said. "Open the door. I need to talk to you."

"Go. Away."

I glanced at Tiffany, who still showed no sign of moving. I'd seen Mo talking with Jessie's mom that day at the gym, but I didn't know how much Tiffany was in the loop about the situation, and it would only have upset Jessie more if I'd started blabbing everything in front of the stepsister who barely tolerated her.

"I know you're mad at me," I said. "You think I told Mo about your, uh, balance problems to be mean. Or, I don't know, maybe you thought I was hoping to move in on your friends and take your place in the gym by forcing you out. Is that it? Is that why you're angry?"

"You know why," Jessie said through the door, but this time her voice was a lot closer; I could tell she was standing on the other side of the door.

"But that's not why I did it," I said. "I *want* you

in the gym. I *want* to train with you. I *want* to be your friend. And friends can't let friends throw everything away, which is what I was afraid you were doing."

"*Friends*"—the emphasis Jessie put on the word made it sound almost like a curse—"don't go behind their friends' backs and spill all their secrets."

"They do if those secrets are dangerous," I said quietly. "They do if they're worried about their friends."

Tiffany was starting to look interested in this whole exchange, and I gave her a wobbly smile to let her know that everything was good, this was just two gym buddies talking shop. I repeated my plea for Jessie to open the door, and finally it cracked open an inch. I saw a sliver of her bloodshot eyes, and I knew she'd been crying.

"Go away," Jessie said. "We're not friends anymore. I don't know if we ever were."

"But—"

"No. Leave me alone, Britt. I don't have anything more to say to you." And with that, she slammed the door in my face.

Tiffany let out a long breath, as though she'd

been watching an intense reality show and it was finally the commercial break. "Wow, she is *mad*," she said. "What was that all about?"

I tried to remember the lie I'd come up with earlier—something about balance problems. "Jessie's having trouble on the beam," I mumbled. "And she doesn't think I should've gone to the coach about it."

"God, you gymnasts argue about the stupidest stuff." Tiffany started to show me to the door, but I shook my head. I already knew the way.

The worst part was that I couldn't blame Jessie at all. It would have been so much easier if I could've just pretended that she was being unreasonable, that it wasn't worth it to be her friend anyway, and that eventually she'd realize how ridiculous she was being. But when I put myself in her shoes, I knew exactly why she was so mad. I'd be angry and hurt and unforgiving, too.

This was the part that my grandmother hadn't talked about, that Atticus hadn't told Scout. If I were Jessie, I'd have hated me. So then, did empathizing with Jessie mean that I should hate myself? I turned the question over and over in my head, until I felt like my brain might explode. Maybe this was how Boo Radley had become such a recluse—he empathized so much with other people's feelings that he started having trouble sorting out his own. There it had been only a few days of this mess for me, and already I was thinking that holing up somewhere else for a while didn't seem like such a bad idea.

Fifteen

Without Jessie at the gym, I found myself eating snack alone at the table where we'd once sat together. Who was I kidding? Even if she were still at the gym, it wasn't like she would've chosen to sit with me. Nobody sits with Boo Radley.

I'd seen the names of the competitors at the upcoming qualifier, and now it was official: Jessie wasn't in it. Apparently, Mo had left the possibility open that Jessie could still come back and try out, but Jessie's mom thought it best if they focused on her health first. At that rate, Jessie wouldn't have been able to try out for the Elite team until fall.

Christina and Noelle gave me dirty looks as they passed. They were eating their snacks by the pro shop again, where Mrs. Flores was working the desk. Before I could give in to second thoughts, I tossed my apple core into the trash and strode over to where they were sitting.

"Can I talk to both of you?" I asked. The people whose opinions I cared about, in order of importance, were Mom, Mo, and Jessie, my only true friend. I'd already tackled all three of those confrontations, with mixed results; now I was ready to take on Christina and Noelle. Considering that we'd never really been friends in the first place, I didn't have much to lose.

"I know you're both mad at me." I noticed that Mrs. Flores seemed to be watching the whole exchange with interest, and I dropped my voice. "Look, maybe we can go somewhere else?"

Christina gave me a haughty look over her cup of yogurt. "Anything you have to say, you can say right here."

"Okay," I said, although I darted one more glance at Mrs. Flores. God only knew what Christina had told her already. "I just wanted to let you know that I understand, and it's okay."

Noelle looked perplexed. "Understand what?"

"Why you didn't say anything about Jessie earlier," I said. "You're not bad friends at all—you were just too close to see it."

"Gee, thanks," Christina said, her voice dripping with sarcasm. "I can't tell you how much it means to me to have your approval."

I was doing my patented foot-in-mouth thing again, but this time I was able to recognize and try to correct it. "No—that's not what I mean. I just don't think you should feel guilty. Christina, you have a ton of pressure on you with this qualifier coming up, and with—" I almost said, *with your mom*—who I knew could be a bit overbearing—but I stopped myself just in time. Although Mrs. Flores had gone back to sorting incoming mail, I knew she could still hear us.

"And Noelle, your parents own a store, right?" I tried to remember what Jessie had told me about Noelle's home life. "I know they need you to help out a lot. And even though you're not competing at the qualifier, you're the only gymnast in the state who got invited to the Nationals, at the training camp. I mean, wow. I can't imagine how awesome that must be, but I know it must be stressful."

Noelle chewed on her bottom lip, as though she was actually thinking about what I was saying, and I felt encouraged. "All I'm trying to say is that *of course* you guys know each other better than I know you. You've been a team for years. But sometimes it takes a person on the outside to see what's going on, and that's what happened with me and Jessie."

I took a deep breath. The last part would be the hardest. "It's not because I don't care about her, or you guys. If anything, it's the opposite. I care so much about being a part of this team that I would hate to see anything bring it down."

It was totally true. It had only been a few short weeks, but more than anything in the world I wanted to feel as if I truly belonged with these three girls. I wanted to be a Texas Twister, through the good and the bad.

Noelle looked at her hands, pulling at a cuticle as she avoided my gaze. Christina stared at me silently, and for a moment I allowed myself to hope. But then her black eyes turned steely, and I knew my entire speech had been useless, even before she opened her mouth.

"At this point," she said, "the only thing bringing this team down is you."

I wondered why I was the villain in her scenario, when I was at least making an attempt to get into their skins and understand how they were feeling. If Christina had taken even a second to put herself in my position, she wouldn't have bothered being mean to me anymore, because she'd have seen that I was already feeling completely defeated.

I tried to convince my grandmother that she should go easy on the homeschooling, considering that the competition season was starting, but she wasn't having it. "You need to exercise your mind as well as your body," she said.

It felt like all I'd been doing for the past few weeks was exercising my mind—mostly, trying to figure out how to get out of all the messes I had gotten myself into. But to Grandma, that wasn't the same as writing an essay about *To Kill a Mockingbird*, so I guessed that was what I had to do.

I was trying to craft a thesis statement about the meaning of the book's title, but I couldn't concentrate. "Grandma, what if you do what you know is the right thing, but it blows up in your face?"

One thing my grandmother was very good at was knowing when I was just malingering (one of her favorite words to describe me) and when something was seriously going on. She seemed to sense that this question was important to me, because she didn't even try to get me back on task.

"Define 'blows up in your face,'" she said.

"Well, like if you lost a friend over it."

She thought about this for a moment. "Are you positive you did the right thing?"

"Yes."

"Then there are two possibilities," she said. "Your friend will realize that, and come back to you, or else, maybe she's not as good a friend as you thought—if she can't see that you acted in the only way you could've."

Adults always said things like that, about how you were better off, blah-blah-blah. But I missed Jessie. She was the only person who'd made me feel welcome when I came to Texas. And sometimes being right didn't feel quite as good as having your friend back.

Before Grandma was forced to prod me, I went back to writing my essay. The title of *To Kill a Mockingbird*, I wrote, referred to a saying that Atticus used, about how it was a sin to kill a mockingbird, because all they did was provide beautiful music, without hurting anyone. Was I the mockingbird in this case? But as much as I hated to admit it, I *had* hurt people—from Christina, when I rubbed it in her face about the full-in, to Noelle, when I took Sparky, to Jessie, when I betrayed her trust.

So then, was Jessie the mockingbird? Had it been a sin to reveal her secret the way I did, when she'd done nothing to me?

I didn't think so. It might have been cheesy, what my grandmother had said about true friends realizing you were acting in their best interests. But it was true. I'd seen a mockingbird with a broken wing, and I had to stop it from trying to fly, in case it got hurt.

A mockingbird couldn't thank me for my help, of course. And maybe that wasn't the point. Maybe the only thing that mattered was that the mockingbird was able to fly away someday, healthy and happy.

Suddenly, analyzing *To Kill a Mockingbird* seemed a lot less complicated than all the stuff swirling in my head.

Sixteen

Cheng had the three of us—minus Jessie now—work out on the floor. We would line up at one corner and, at Cheng's signal, flip and tumble our way to the opposite corner. Then we would start the whole process over, going back and forth with our passes until he determined we'd practiced enough.

For me, it felt like one of those classic word problems: a farmer needs to get his chicken, fox, and grain over to the other side of the river, but the fox can never be alone with the chicken, and the chicken can never be alone with the grain. In this case, I was the chicken. If I was left with the fox (Christina), she'd eat me alive. If I was left with the grain (Noelle) . . . Well, it wasn't really like I would eat her. So maybe it was more like I was left with *two* foxes.

Christina landed her double twist and went to take her place in line behind me, nudging my shoulder as she passed. I knew it was on purpose. There was only an entire *gym* full of space for her to walk around me, so there was no reason to come that close. I tried to ignore her, but I couldn't help taking a small step forward to put more space between us. I watched Noelle land her tumbling run (feet perfectly planted on the mat, waist not piked too far down, of course) before preparing to take my turn again.

At least the girls were now just cold and quiet. A few days before, when the incident with Jessie was still fresh, Christina would whisper nasty things if we happened to be standing near each other at the chalk bowl or something. She whispered to me about how it was all my fault, about how much better off the Texas Twisters had been without me, and about how I should go back to Ohio.

I'd be lying if I said it didn't hurt. When I thought back to my first day at the gym, how nervous I'd been, how much I'd wanted these girls to like me, I felt this pain in my chest that was something like the burn I got after eating Grandma's spicy chili, but different. It was deeper. When I'd first moved to Austin, I had thought that these girls were all sticks in the mud who could use some lightening up, and that I was just the girl to help them do it. Now it seemed as if all my attempts at fun had been misguided, and when it came time to deal with something really serious, I'd messed it up.

Before Christina set off on her next tumbling run, Cheng told her to try the tucked full-in she'd been struggling with.

"You'll spot me, right?" she asked, and her voice shook slightly. So the Great Christina was human, after all.

"I'll be right here," Cheng said, but he didn't agree to spot her, exactly. He obviously wanted her to try it without his help, although he'd be there in case she needed him.

Christina's back was to me, so I couldn't see her face, but I could tell by the way she clenched and unclenched her fists at her sides that she was nervous. Even though we were far from being friends, I found myself cheering her on—in my head, of course; I didn't want to get her Glare of Death again.

"Come on, Christina," Noelle said. "You can do this."

"Just on the floor?" Christina asked.

Cheng nodded. "You ready," he said.

Her shoulders moved up and down in an exaggerated motion, as if she were taking a deep breath, and then she stretched her fingers reflexively before straightening her arms at her sides, with one foot flat on the ground and the other pointed in front of her.

Once she took off, it was like everything happened in slow motion. She was running, springing into her round-off back handspring, and then she was in the air, her body flipping and twisting. I knew when she was still in midair that she wasn't going to make it, and in those stretched-out moments it felt almost as if I should *say* something, *do* something to help her. I saw Cheng moving toward her, but everything felt impossibly delayed.

In reality, it was only a millisecond before Christina crashed onto the floor, her feet touching the mat an instant before her head did, her body folding at the waist. The only thing that stopped her from face-planting was Cheng's intervention; he took hold of her arm and pulled her upper body away from the floor.

That was why it could be nerve-racking to do a skill for the first time without a spot. Your trainer might have been there, but you had to be realistic. He was not always going to be able to get there in time to save you.

Noelle and I rushed over to Christina. At that moment, I wasn't thinking about Jessie or the fact that Christina hated me. I just wanted to make sure she was okay.

Mrs. Flores also came running over from the parents' viewing section, and she bent over Christina. I heard her exclaiming over her daughter. As soon as she realized that it had looked scarier than it actually was, her tone changed and she stood up.

"The qualifier is in a week," she hissed at Christina. "If you can't get this, you won't make Elite. Do you want that? To watch everyone leave you behind?"

Whoa. I hadn't transitioned yet from my concern about Christina, but apparently her mother had. Christina was rising to her feet now, and her mom towered over her in her alligator-skin heels, lecturing her about the importance of doing something over and over again until you got it right.

"The new girl can do this move," Christina's mom was saying as she led a stunned Christina off to the side. I didn't know if the dazed look was the aftereffect of the fall, or if it was surprise at her mother's attack. "When are *you* going to?"

I couldn't believe that, at one point, I'd actually been jealous of Christina's relationship with her mother. I'd envied the fact that her mom was always at the gym and seemed to care about her daughter's gymnastics, unlike my mom, who was caught up in her own work. But I realized that my mother didn't really care whether I moved up a level or not, as long as I was happy and I tried my best. I don't know if I could have handled her breathing down my neck all the time.

I turned to Noelle. "Man," I said loudly, "I wish I had half of Christina's grace."

She wrinkled her forehead in confusion. "What?"

"Have you seen her full turn on beam? It's, like, the most beautiful thing I've ever seen. The judges love that kind of stuff, but I suck at it."

"Um . . . okay."

I continued undaunted. "I mean, you can *learn* how to do tumbling passes, you know? Anyone can do a piked full-in after a bit of practice. But if you're not a good dancer, forget it. It's so much harder to work on that."

Noelle glanced over at Mrs. Flores and Christina, who weren't bothering to disguise the fact that they were listening. Finally, she seemed to get it. "Oh, yeah," she said. "Christina's always been awesome at the artistic part of gymnastics."

"So lucky," I said. "She'll get that piked full-in by next week; but me? I don't think I'll ever learn how to do a perfect arabesque."

Mrs. Flores had her hand on Christina's shoulder. She gave it a squeeze. "Let me buy you a Gatorade at the concession," she said. "I'm sure Cheng would understand if you took a five-minute break."

Christina turned to leave with her mom, but she shot me a look over her shoulder. I couldn't tell if she was grateful for my intervention, but it didn't matter. I'd just done what I hoped someone else might do for me—been a friend.

Cheng gave us all a short break, and I headed in to the locker room. I don't know how long I sat on the bench, lost in my own thoughts, before Christina and Noelle came in. Christina was holding her Gatorade, and I watched them approach like those slow zombies in the movies. I knew they were going to tear the flesh from my limbs and snack on my intestines, but I was glued to the spot. I couldn't do anything but stare as they stopped right in front of me.

"We—" Noelle began.

"Listen—" Christina said.

They glanced at each other. "Let me go first," Christina said. "I'm the one who's been such a heinous jerk. Britt, we want to apologize."

"Apologize?" I repeated, like an idiot. Surely I must have heard wrong. *They* wanted to apologize to *me*?

"You were right," Noelle said. "About everything. Jessie's been acting weirder and weirder for a while, and if we had bothered to look closer, we would've seen it wasn't just stress about the qualifier. I don't know if we didn't want to see it—"

"—Or we were just too busy with our own drama," Christina broke in, shaking her head in disgust. "Honestly, I was so wrapped up in my competition with you that I barely noticed Jessie.

If it hadn't been for you, nobody would've ever spoken up."

I wondered if this was a dream, or if there was a way to ask them to repeat all the nice stuff they were saying to me into a tape recorder so that I could play it back whenever I started thinking they hated me.

"Jessie asked me not to tell anyone," I said. "I should've handled it differently—made her tell someone or whatever. I shouldn't have brought it up at your sleepover."

Christina waved her hand. "I was being a brat about that sleepover, anyway," she said. "I'm sorry I didn't invite you."

"You did," I said, "eventually."

"We should have another sleepover soon," Noelle said, "and maybe we should skip Truth or Dare."

I bit my lip. "It won't be the same without Jessie, though."

Noelle drew her eyebrows together. "Why wouldn't we invite Jessie?"

"I just don't think she'll come," I said. "She's really mad at me. I doubt she'll ever forgive me."

It might've been different if Jessie and I had been friends for years, if we'd grown up together and gone through Girl Scouts together and told countless secrets to each other. Maybe then, Jessie would someday have realized I'd been acting out of concern. But what did we have holding our friendship together, really, except for a couple of conversations during our snack break and one homework help session?

Christina and Noelle glanced at each other.

"Let us take care of that," Noelle said.

I shrugged. I doubted there was much they could do, but it was nice of them to want to try. Turning back to my locker, I took out a roll of athletic tape and started wrapping my ankle.

"Are you hurt?" Christina asked. It was going to take a while to get used to hearing her speak without any sarcasm in her voice, but it was definitely a welcome change.

"Nah," I said. "But since we're going back out on the floor, I thought I'd tape up my ankle just in case. For some reason, I've been landing my passes with more weight on this side, and I don't want to put any extra stress on it."

"Don't take this the wrong way," Noelle said. "But you'd better not. Mo and Cheng have very strong feelings about using bandages or tape in practice."

"We're not allowed to use tape?"

"Only if you're hurt," Noelle said. "They think that using it when you're not is just a crutch that weakens your body."

A few weeks earlier, I would've assumed that they were messing with me, making stuff up in order to get me in trouble or make me look stupid. But I believed them now. I started unwinding the tape, wincing as I ripped off a strip around my anklebone. "Thanks," I said.

"Any time," Noelle said. "We're teammates, aren't we?"

Seventeen

Excitement was in the air on the day of the qualifier. I climbed to the top of the bleachers with Noelle, since neither of us was competing. I don't think I'd ever just sat and watched a gymnastics meet before. Even back in Ohio, once when I'd gotten really sick in the middle of a competition, I'd waited out the rest of it in a back room with my head between my knees.

"This is fun, right?" Noelle asked. We were both wearing our new team jackets, which Mo had ordered in a bright red with white stitching across the back advertising our gym. The logo depicted a gymnast with a bunch of swirls around her, as though she were a cyclone.

"Totally," I said. "It's weird, though. Don't you feel like we should be out there, somehow?"

"Yeah." Noelle grew quiet; I was sure she had the same images running through her head that I did: sitting perfectly still while someone spritzed hair spray all over your hair; the premeet pep talk from your coach; the adrenaline rush as you walked out onto the floor for the first time, taking in all the equipment that had been set up and the other teams as they began to stretch.

In order to qualify for Elite competition, Christina had to get a certain all-around score. Noelle said that she'd gotten scores that high before, at a competition last year, but it hadn't been an official qualifier, so it hadn't counted.

"Well, if she's done it before, she can do it again," I said.

Noelle nodded, but she looked a little worried. I guess when you'd seen a friend compete at ten separate meets, the fact that she got such a great score at one of them wasn't a big confidence-booster.

"She's got the full-in now," I pointed out.

Christina had gotten much more consistent at performing that skill in the last week. I liked to think it was because of the advice I'd given her, which she was now finally willing to listen to—but I knew it was probably all Cheng's general awesomeness. He didn't talk much, but my experience working with him over the past couple of weeks had taught me that he didn't have to. He had a way of showing you what you needed to do in the fewest steps possible, so that it seemed almost effortless. One minute you were hitting a brick wall, and the next minute you were flying. It was incredible.

An announcement came over the loudspeaker, asking everyone to stand for the national anthem.

After the anthem, we sat back down. The program said that Christina was in the first group, which started on vault. I knew she would be relieved by drawing Olympic order, which goes: vault, then bars, then beam, and ends with floor. She likes to get vault out of the way early, so that she can focus on the events she says actually interest her.

I saw my mom at the bottom of the bleachers searching for me, and I waved to let her know where we were. She'd dropped Noelle and me off in front and then circled around the parking lot to find a space. It was totally insane how crowded places could get for these things.

"It sucks your mom couldn't be here," I said to Noelle. I realized I'd never met any of Noelle's family.

She shrugged. "It's hard with the store. My older brothers can't run it on their own, so my parents pretty much always have to be there."

"I didn't know you had brothers."

"Four of them." Noelle rolled her eyes. "The twins are eight, and then Radu and Mihai are both in high school. And before you ask, no, they are *not* cute."

Like I'd have been interested. I still thought boys were, for the most part, complete wastes of time. Who wanted to go to the movies with some kid who'd rather tell fart jokes than watch the thing he'd paid eight dollars to see? It was stupid.

"Cute like Scott, you mean?" I teased, waggling my eyebrows.

As expected, Noelle flushed a little.

"What's the deal with you and him, anyway?" I asked.

"There's no *deal*," she said. "I get that he's older

than me, and it could never happen. It's just . . . I like dreaming about it, I guess."

"Has he ever actually spoken to you? I mean, other than—" I didn't want to remind Noelle of the time I'd taken her stuffed animal. Not when we were finally getting along. "Other than a little bit here and there?"

"Not yet," she said, lowering her voice as my mom reached our row. "But someday."

"Hi, girls." My mom smiled at us, unaware of our topic of discussion—which was a good thing, because I didn't even want to think about the way she would have squealed with delight if she'd thought I was talking about *boys*.

I knew it wasn't easy for her to spend her whole Saturday here when she still had a lot to do to get the day care ready. But she was making an effort, and so was I. I told her that I'd be happy to spend the next day going through kids' toys with her in exchange for her coming to the meet.

"Hi, Mrs. Morgan," Noelle said. Sometimes I still felt a little jealous of my mother's obvious affection for Noelle, but I knew my mother cared about me. And honestly, it was hard not to be completely charmed by Noelle. She was good at everything, but she didn't have a big head about it.

And then it was Christina's turn at vault, and we all grew quiet. She ran down the runway, did a round-off onto the springboard, and then flipped backward to push off the vaulting table into a full twist. It wasn't at quite the level of difficulty of some of the other girls' vaults, but she landed fairly solidly.

I didn't pretend to care about the other competitors. I was really only there to watch Christina. So, while some short, mousy-looking girl got set up for her vault, I turned to Noelle.

"I can't wait for the Classic. I really want to get back out there on the floor. It feels like I haven't competed in forever."

Noelle sighed. "I know. I'm not competing at the Classic, although there's Nationals later this summer. I want to go so badly I can taste it, but . . ."

I waited a few seconds for her to finish her sentence; when she didn't, I prompted her: "But what?"

"It costs a lot of money," she said. "They're in Philadelphia, so there's the flight, and the hotel, and the new leotards. . . ."

"You've gotta go," I said. "If you don't, who's going to be my competition?"

I hadn't meant to make it sound like I didn't think Christina would qualify—because I totally did—or like I didn't consider her competition. Even though, if I had been honest, I really saw Noelle as my biggest rival . . . at least, gymnasticswise. Obviously, she was the best, since she'd been hand-selected to compete at Nationals. Christina—if she qualified—and I would have to score big at the upcoming Classic for that privilege.

Noelle smiled distractedly.

Then a girl took a particularly nasty fall on the bars, and we both winced.

"I wouldn't want to be feeling like her in an hour or so," I said. "One time I belly-flopped on the mat like that, and I didn't think it hurt so much at the time, but by the time I got home, my muscles were all stiff and sore."

Noelle and I traded gymnastics war stories while we waited for Christina to rotate to her next event. Neither one of us had ever been seriously injured. The worst I'd ever had was a sprained ankle; Noelle had broken a few fingers and pulled a muscle in her leg.

Then Christina was on the bars, and we watched as she swung gracefully back and forth, switching between the low and high bars with ease. She really did have the most beautiful lines. I wondered what her secret was—metal rods implanted in her legs, to keep them so perfectly straight?

She stuck her dismount, and I finally let myself breathe. I knew Noelle was doing the same.

"Next is beam," she said. "That's one of Christina's best events. So far, she's doing awesome."

I couldn't wait to get out on the competition floor again. That was when I really came alive. There was just something about the atmosphere, the pressure, the other girls in the background competing for the same thing . . . It always revved me up.

Okay, so I'd been known to get *too* revved up and totally choke in a crunch. But I was getting better. And it's better to have too much energy than too little, right?

My mom must have been thinking the same thing, because she leaned over and said, "Do you remember the time you fell off the beam three times in one competition, and the last time, you actually slapped the beam, you were so frustrated?"

"Mom!" I didn't need for Noelle to hear a high-light reel of my greatest misses.

"What? You were only seven years old. It was cute."

"Losing is not *cute*, Mom." Out of the corner of my eye, I saw Noelle smirk. Note to self: whenever I do get to meet the Onestis, ask them to regale me with embarrassing stories about Noelle.

When Christina finally got to the beam, I could see what Noelle meant. Sometimes you hear commentators for gymnastics meets say that a gymnast "works the beam like it's floor." (Actually, you hear it all the time, because apparently, gymnastics commentators are like those old Barbie dolls you pull a string on and hear the same stupid phrase over and over.) Well, that's exactly what I thought of when I saw Christina. She danced from one end of the beam to the other as though she had no idea that it was only four inches wide or that she had a long way to fall. She might not have felt so fearless, but I could see she had more courage than she gave herself credit for.

The audience applauded when she landed her series of flip-flops into a front aerial linked to an immediate sheep jump; this meant that they were watching her and not the other girl who was performing on floor at the same time. Every now and then, the other girl's floor music was perfectly matched up to Christina's movements, so that it looked almost as if Christina was leaping and twirling to the beat. For a moment, I felt as though there were something magical in the building.

"She's going to qualify," I said. "She has to. She's having the best competition of her life."

But Noelle was more cautious. "She's doing great, but floor is next. She loves all the dancing parts, but that one tumbling pass is still not a sure thing."

"Then why throw it in there at all? Why risk a mistake?"

"Christina had to improve either her vault difficulty or her floor difficulty to be competitive," Noelle explained. "Cheng decided it was easier to upgrade her first tumbling pass to a full-in than to try the new vault, since that's the event that scares her the most."

It felt like forever before the girls rotated to their last events. Christina was competing toward the middle of the pack, which wasn't a terrible position to be in. Usually, girls competing toward the beginning of the rotation get scored lower, because the judges want to give themselves room to raise scores as the competition progresses. You don't want to give an almost perfect score to the first girl and then have the next one hit her routine out of the park, because then all the scores get inflated. So it was better for the competitors to go toward the end, but middle wasn't all that bad; in this case, it meant that Christina wouldn't have to wait around as long, with all that time for her muscles to get cold and for her to psych herself out.

I was on the edge of my seat as the girl before Christina took her place on the floor, performing a decent routine to some classical music I'd never heard before. Somebody, punch me in the face if I ever do a routine to boring dead people playing harps and stuff.

The girl finished her routine with a flourish, and I felt my heart jump into my throat. This was it. The big moment. I was surprised at how badly I wanted Christina to qualify, even though she'd been my archnemesis just a few days ago.

There was a rustling next to me. I glanced over, annoyed at whoever was choosing *this* moment to get up and go grab a hot dog and a bag of chips. But then I forgot about hot dogs, about Christina, and about the competition.

"Jessie?"

"You didn't think I'd miss it, did you?" She smiled brightly at Noelle and me.

My mother raised her eyebrows at me over the top of Jessie's head. I'd ended up telling her everything that was going on and had expressed my confusion over why Jessie's mom had chosen to pull her out of the gym right before what would have been the biggest competition of her life. My mom had said that someday, when I had children of my own, I'd understand. Gymnastics might have been our dream, but making sure we were healthy and happy was our parents' dream, and it had to come first. I pretended to gag when she said stuff like that, but deep down, I liked to hear it.

"You're just in time," Noelle said. She didn't look nearly as surprised as I was. Maybe she'd just known that Jessie would show up to support her teammate, no matter what. "Christina's about to go on."

Right on cue, Christina's music started, a swirling Latin beat that wasn't too fast but still managed to sound cool. Christina was in her starting pose, one arm crooked behind her back and the other held high in a gesture that almost screamed, *Watch what I'm about to do.*

The big tumbling pass was right at the beginning. It would have made more impact if it had been the last pass, but by the end of the routine you were usually totally out of breath, so sometimes it made sense to play it safe then. Cheng had said that if Christina got more comfortable with the move, they might change it, but for now it was in the first ten seconds, so that she could concentrate all her energy and focus on landing that skill.

She danced into the corner, placing her feet with the heels just inside the white line. I saw her shoulders rise and fall, and then she was off.

Her back handspring was much better. I knew as soon as she hit it that she would have enough power to fling herself backward into the double flip with a single twist. The question was whether she would stick it. . . . I held my breath as I watched her body flip through the air.

The sound of her feet hitting the springboard-loaded mat could be heard throughout the building. It wasn't until she threw both of her arms up in a triumphant salute that it fully registered.

"She did it!" I cried. "She did it! She did it!"

But Noelle was biting her lip. "No. She stepped out of bounds," she said. "That's going to cost her a couple of tenths. And if it throws her off her game, it might cost her even more."

I'd been so focused on the fact that Christina was up and on her feet that I hadn't even noticed where she'd landed. But sure enough, her back leg was way over the white line.

I did some quick calculations: Christina needed a 9.5 or better on this routine to secure her Elite status. It was totally possible, but depending on how much they decided to deduct for the out-of-bounds step, it might not happen.

Christina kept a brave face on, getting through the rest of her routine with only minor shakiness on one of her leaps and finishing with a relatively conservative double twist. That 9.5 was looking a little further out of reach.

"They can't take more than one-tenth for that step, right?" I asked as we waited for her score. "That would be totally unfair."

My gaze caught Jessie's at that moment, and I quickly looked away. She was probably the last person who wanted to weigh in on what was fair, considering that this was supposed to be her competition, too. I wished I could've detected any forgiveness in those eyes, but I was too afraid of the alternative to look really closely.

They flashed her score, and we all cheered. Apparently, they'd seen her grace and beauty and knew that she deserved the 9.5.

Noelle and I grinned at each other, and I automatically smiled at Jessie before reality hit again with a thud. Christina was an Elite now, which meant that all of us were officially on the Elite team . . . except for Jessie. She would still train with us, but she was a Level Ten. There would always be two different competitions: one with the three of us, and one with just her.

"Jessie . . ."

But she shook her head, as if she didn't want to hear it. Even though it was awesome that Christina and Noelle and I were cool now, I realized how much I missed having Jessie as my best friend in the group. Christina and Noelle were clearly tight—they were always going over to each other's houses and giggling about something that had happened in school, since they were in the same grade. I had hoped that Jessie and I could've also been like that, but now it was too late.

"Can I talk to you?" she asked me in a low voice. "Outside?"

I nodded, trying not to get my hopes up. It was possible that Jessie wanted to have an I-will-always-hate-you-so-please-don't-even-look-at-me kind of conversation, but as I excused myself from Noelle and my mom and followed Jessie down the bleachers, I tried to feel encouraged. At least she wanted to talk.

Eighteen

May in Texas was really hot, although there was a little breeze sometimes that shook some of the trees and provided relief. Jessie and I sat on a bench under one of those trees. I waited for her to speak.

"Noelle and Christina said you feel really guilty about what happened," Jessie said.

So, they had talked to her. I'd wondered what they'd meant by "taking care of it." One thing was for sure—I was glad they were on my side now.

"A part of me says that you should be," Jessie

continued. "I told you a lot of stuff I usually keep to myself, about my true feelings about the way I look and how inferior I feel to the rest of you guys in gymnastics. You all make it look so easy. Even though Christina has some trouble with the harder moves, she just looks so *beautiful* up there that of course the judges are going to give her high scores for her long lines."

I tried to imagine how I would have felt if I had spilled all my secret fears—that I wouldn't fit in anywhere, that I'd put my foot in my mouth so much that my only option was to become a mute, that my mother would see some adorable little three-year-old orphan at her day care and think, *Hey, this one's cuter than the one I've got at home, and better behaved, too.* If I'd told that to Jessie and she'd blabbed about it during a game of Truth or Dare, I'd probably have been pretty mad, too.

"I really trusted you," Jessie said. "And I feel like you betrayed that."

If anyone had tried to stand between me and my gymnastics by going behind my back and talking to my coaches, I'd have been livid. I would've thrown a huge tantrum in the middle of the gym and accused everyone of conspiring against me. I definitely wouldn't have quietly packed my stuff and left, the way Jessie did.

I would have hoped that I had friends who cared enough about me to stand up and say something if they thought I was hurting myself. I wanted to say that in my defense, but I sensed that Jessie wasn't finished yet.

"I just wish maybe at the very least you'd talked to me about the whole thing," she said, "instead of talking to other people."

She was right. I could see that now. But at the time, it had seemed as if Jessie was in such denial about herself that I couldn't trust her to actually listen to anything I said. Still, I realized that I should've given her the chance, so that when I did go to Mo and the other girls, at least I'd allowed her to handle it herself.

"You said a *part* of you thinks I should feel guilty," I said, my voice almost a whisper. I couldn't look Jessie in the eyes as I traced the diamond-wire pattern of the bench with my finger. "What about the other part?"

"The other part of me knows you did the right thing."

I did look at Jessie then, and I felt like I was

seeing my old friend. She gave me a small smile. "I still don't think I have anorexia or something, like this woman my parents are taking me to seems to think. She's a psychologist, and I have to talk to her once a week now, to make sure I'm not falling back into my pattern of 'irrational thoughts.'"

She noticed my confused look and laughed. "That's what they call it when you think you're really fat but you're not, and you think everyone's judging you but they're not. She thinks I'm my own worst enemy."

Sometimes, I thought, we were all our own worst enemies. That sounds superdeep, I know, but it's true. Christina lets her own fear stand in her way, Noelle worries about everything, Jessie feels insecure, and I . . . well, I'm insecure, too, I guess. I think that people won't like me, so I decide to do outrageous things that will *make* them notice me, even though I know as I'm doing them that I'm only making it worse.

Wow. It was like I was having a minibreak-through, and I wasn't even paying anyone to tell me this kind of stuff.

"Anyway," Jessie went on, "I know things got out of control. Somehow, I just told myself, if you lose all this weight by the qualifier, you'll win. And then that number started getting bigger and bigger."

"I'm sorry that I messed up the qualifier for you," I said. "Now you'll have to wait for the next one."

Jessie shrugged. "I wasn't ready. If I had competed today and lost, I would've crawled into a hole. It's better that I take some extra time for myself before I have to worry about something so huge."

"You are coming back to practice, though, right? We've missed you."

"Wild horses couldn't stop me," she said.

"So, what are you doing this summer?" I asked. "School gets out soon, huh?"

"What do you think I'm doing?" Jessie grinned at me. "Gym, gym, and more gym. But we always make some time to have fun, too. Once a summer, Mrs. Flores usually takes us all to the beach. And there's a carnival that comes to town."

"That sounds fun." I thought wistfully of the carnival back home in Ohio, where the Ferris wheel was so old that it just had those little benches with a single metal rod to hold you in place. I used to love to go on it with Dionne and shake the bench, just to mess with her. But then one time she threw up all over me, so I guess I learned my lesson.

"And my mom was so happy you helped me with my algebra homework, you're welcome over anytime." Jessie looked down at her hands. Her fingers were entwined with the diamond cutouts, although I noticed that she didn't go past the first knuckle. That was a good thing. I'd gotten my fingers stuck in those holes before. "We're still—"

The door opened, and Noelle and Christina walked cautiously toward us, as though making sure that we weren't about to gouge each other's eyes out or something, with them caught in the middle. Christina had her gym bag slung over her shoulder and was wearing her nylon jacket and pants over her leotard.

"What's up?" she asked.

"What's up?" Jessie repeated incredulously. "What's *up*? You're an Elite gymnast now, that's what's up!"

Christina flushed. "I didn't want to say anything, but . . ." She let out a big whoop, pumping her fist in the air like she was that boxer Rocky, who always seemed like he was down but then always came through in the end.

"We're walking over to the awards now," Noelle said. "You guys want to come?" She glanced from Jessie to me, as if trying to gauge what had gone down between us.

I smiled at Jessie to show that we were cool, and she put her arm around me. "We're down," she said. "As long as it's not one of those where they give ribbons out to, like, sixteenth place."

"It's not," Christina promised.

"And if it is, you won't have to stick around that long," Noelle pointed out. "We'll just grab Christina's gold medal and head out to lunch!"

"Gold? That's awesome!" I knew Christina had scored high enough to qualify for Elite, but I hadn't known she'd gotten the all-around gold, too.

We walked to the building where they were holding the awards ceremony, which I knew would be all decked out in balloons and crepe paper. You'd think they'd figure out a way to decorate these things other than like a birthday party, but whatever.

"I was telling Britt about our summer plans," Jessie said. "The beach, and the carnival . . ."

"Oh, God, the carnival!" Christina laughed. "Don't eat the Elephant Ears. Seriously, they're so greasy they'll make your stomach hurt for days."

"Is the Ferris wheel one of those old kinds, with the benches?" I asked.

Noelle frowned. "I can't remember. Why?"

"Oh, no reason . . ." I said. I probably wouldn't play that trick on them, because I felt like I knew better now than to do that. I was able to put myself in their shoes and to realize that sometimes being scared wasn't fun. Before, I would've just assumed that everyone liked to be teased. But now I knew that part of being friends was knowing the limits, and knowing when to be serious and when to let loose.

As we walked side by side, feeling the breeze on our faces and knowing that we had an afternoon of celebratory lunch and postcompetition high to enjoy before starting another week of bone-pounding practice, we were definitely more than just teammates.

We were friends.

Gymnastics glossary

aerial: A cartwheel done without the use of hands for support on the floor

arabesque: A dance element in which one leg is on the floor and one leg lifted backward toward the ceiling to form an extended line

beam: A horizontal, raised apparatus that is four inches wide, sixteen feet in length, and approximately four feet off the floor; on this, gymnasts perform a series of dance moves and acrobatic skills.

blind landing: A landing in which the gymnast ends up facing forward, sometimes away from the apparatus, and she cannot see the floor before landing

difficulty level: A way of measuring what a skill is worth in the gymnastics code of points, or how hard a skill is to execute

floor: A carpeted surface measuring forty feet square, over springs and wooden boards. Also the term for the only event in which a gymnast performs a routine set to music; the routine is ninety seconds in length, and composed of dance and acrobatic elements.

full-in: Two flips in the air with the first flip featuring a 360-degree twist

full turn: A 360-degree turn on one leg, performed on floor and beam

grips: Strips of leather placed on a gymnast's hand to prevent calluses and allow for a better grip on the uneven bars

handspring: A move in which a gymnast starts on both feet, jumps to a position supporting her body with just her two hands on the floor, and then pushes off to land on her feet again. This can be done forward or backward, and is typically used to start or connect an acrobatic series.

Junior Elite: The level before Senior Elite, as designated by regulations of the governing body of gymnastics. Junior Elite gymnasts are not allowed to compete in the Olympics.

layout: A maneuver completed in the air with hands held against the body and a pencil-straight overall position; flipping can be forward or backward, and the move ends with the gymnast standing on both feet again.

pike: A position in which the body is bent double at the hips, with legs straight and toes pointed

press handstand: A move beginning on the floor with legs in a straddle position and all of the weight on the hands. The entire body is raised over the head and moves from a straddle position into a straight-body handstand.

punch front: A jump from a position on both feet into a forward-flipping somersault in which the gymnast lands again on both feet, still facing forward

round-off: A move that begins like a cartwheel, but in which the legs swing together overhead, and the gymnast finishes facing in the opposite direction

scale: A position in which one leg is raised high into the air while the other leg is firmly planted on the ground. Ideally, this position ends in a 180-degree vertical split.

Senior Elite: The level after Junior Elite, as designated by regulations of the governing body of gymnasts. In women's artistic gymnastics, a gymnast must be turning sixteen years of age within the calendar year during which the competition takes place to become a Senior Elite.

sheep jump: A move in which the gymnast jumps into the air, throws her head back until it touches her feet for a split second, and then returns to a straight-body position to land on both feet

split: A position in which one leg is stretched in front of the body and the other behind

standing full twist: A move that begins in a stationary position on both feet, followed by a jump into a flip with a 360-degree twist in the air (usually in a tucked position with legs bent at a ninety-degree angle) before a landing on both feet. Typically, this move is completed on floor or beam.

straddle: A position in which the right leg is stretched out to the right side of the body and the left leg is stretched out to the left, as the gymnast faces forward

stuck dismount: A move in which a gymnast executes a landing with both feet firmly planted on the ground and no wobbling occurs.

tuck: A position in which the knees are folded in toward the chest at a ninety-degree angle, with the waist bent, creating the shape of a ball

tumbling passes: A series of connected acrobatic moves required in a floor-exercise routine

uneven bars: (often, just "bars") One of four apparatuses in women's artistic gymnastics. Bars features the apparatus on which women perform mostly using their upper-body strength. This event consists of two rails placed at an uneven level; one bar acts as the high bar and the other as the low bar. Both bars are flexible, helping the gymnast to connect skills from one to the other.

vault: A runway of approximately eighty feet in length, leading to the springboard and a padded table at one end. The gymnast runs full speed toward the table, using the springboard to launch herself onto it; she then pushes off with her hands, moving into a series of flips and/or twists before landing on the mat behind the table.

Yurchenko vault: A vaulting move that begins with a round-off onto the springboard, followed by a back handspring onto the table; the gymnast then pushes off into a series of flips and/or twists before landing on the mat. This style of vault was named after Soviet gymnast Natalia Yurchenko.

Don't miss the next novel in

One

Ever since Mr. Van Buren had used the term *muscle memory* in science class, I'd been obsessed with the idea. The concept wasn't new to me, but now I had a name for it. I'd been doing gymnastics practically since I could walk, so it was easy to believe that there were memories buried deep in the muscles of my legs and feet that were way older than the memory of the first time I ate watermelon, or saw the ocean.

Now, standing at the very corner of the floor mat on my tiptoes, ready to launch into a tumbling pass, it wasn't like I had time to consider all of the philosophical implications of this idea. But that was the whole point of muscle memory—I didn't *have* to think. It was just there, in the flex of my ankles, the texture of the mat under the balls of my feet as I sprang into a run across the floor, the stretch of my calves as I kick-started the momentum that would carry me flipping from one end of the mat to the other. When I landed my double pike, my feet planted firmly and my hips square with my shoulders, it was like déjà vu. My body had been in this exact position so many times that I lay in bed at night and re-created it, until it was almost like I fell asleep flipping.

Cheng nodded his head and twirled his finger, his signal for *again*. With Cheng, you learned that this was all you were going to get. He was not the most vocal of coaches, and would never be the one to sweep you up in a bear hug on national television and scream, "You did it! You did it!" but he showed his satisfaction in other ways. Mostly, it was by telling you to keep working.

"Man," Britt said, rubbing chalk on the bottoms of her feet as she joined me at the corner of the floor. "Hasn't he heard of the Thirteenth Amendment? I'm pretty sure it abolished slavery."

I smiled just enough to let Britt know I'd heard

her, but not so much that it might have looked like I was participating in the conversation. Britt was the newest gymnast at Texas Twisters, and when she first got there, she had made a lot of waves because of how outspoken she was. She worked harder than she let on, and she was more determined now than she used to be, but sometimes she still joked around. It could be fun, but pretty much the only thing that scared me more than spiders was getting into trouble, so I tried not to give the coaches any reason to call me out.

Christina had been stretching on the side, but came over to line up behind Britt. "It can't be slavery if you're paying to be here," she said, rolling her eyes.

I preferred to avoid thinking about the dollars adding up and multiplying for every day that I trained at Texas Twisters. My parents never talked about how much it cost, exactly, but I knew being an Elite gymnast was not cheap.

"Noelle," Christina said, jabbing me in the shoulder, "are you going to go, or what?"

I blinked, realizing that somehow I'd allowed myself to get distracted, when that was the last thing I should have been doing as the competitive season started. Squaring myself up on a corner of the blue mat, I took another deep breath and allowed muscle memory to take over.

When we'd finished stretching at the end of practice, our coach Mo called all of us together. Adrenaline made my heart race; I knew what this would be about. The U.S. Junior National Championships were coming up in a few months—so close it was like reaching out to grab the high bar after a big release skill. I only hoped I could catch it.

Mo surveyed the four of us: me, Christina, Britt, and Jessie, who'd returned full-time to practice but wasn't planning on trying for Nationals. She'd taken some time off to cope with her eating disorder, and was still dealing with it. We had all been walking on eggshells, afraid of saying the wrong thing, but she mostly didn't talk about it.

Christina was examining her brand-new manicure as though this meeting didn't have anything to do with the most important event in her career so far. She'd just qualified for Elite competition two weeks ago, and there was no guarantee that she'd be eligible to participate in the qualifying event this early, much less in the Nationals. I could tell she was trying to act like she didn't care, but how could she not? This was *the* competition of the year, the one that determined whether or not you made the National team and got to compete internationally. They featured new up-and-comers from that competition in the biggest gymnastics magazines in the world. It was huge.

Even Britt wasn't pretending it was all a joke, the way she sometimes did. Her blue eyes were sparkling, and she was clenching and unclenching her fists at her side as though she could actually reach out and touch that National Championship gold medal. I felt a spurt of competitiveness. Nothing against Britt, but I'd be more than happy for her to take home the silver and leave the gold for me.

"You know this is important time," Mo said. Mo wasn't a talker, either, but compared to Cheng, she might as well have been Oprah. Maybe that was why Cheng was happy to spot us on the floor and help us with vault timers while Mo handled the business side of things.

"U.S. Classic is in one month," Mo continued, referring to the event that would determine whether Britt and Christina would go to Nationals. I'd already qualified earlier in the year, through a training camp. "Here, you are not against each other. You are together. Understand?"

Britt and Christina exchanged a look, but both nodded. It had been a little tense the past few months, until we decided that Britt could be just as much a friend as a threat, and I knew that Mo didn't want us to be distracted by that kind of drama as we started training for the Classic.

Only a handful of gymnasts qualified for Nationals through a training camp, and it was a relief to be one of them, since it meant that I could focus completely on that goal without worrying about the Classic. Every year, Coach Piserchia held these training camps where he invited gymnasts from all over the country to participate. This year, I'd been the only representative from Texas Twisters, and it was one of the most nerve-racking experiences of my life. Coach Piserchia was officially retired from individual coaching, but he still played a huge role in deciding who would represent our country at World Championships and at the Olympics, so impressing him was majorly important.

Now, Mo handed each of us a thick envelope. "Make sure parents get this," she said. "They need to come to meeting at gym, too."

It was irrational, since everyone had gotten an envelope, and surely *everyone* couldn't be in trouble, but like I said, I get paranoid. I hated the thought of people being mad at me, so as I looked down at the sealed envelope filled with papers intended for my parents' eyes only, all kinds of scenarios started whirling through my head. Maybe it was an assessment of my abilities up to this point, and Mo wanted to break it to them gently that any chance of my making the Olympics someday was very, very slim. Or maybe Cheng had noticed my distraction earlier that day and added it to a list of times when I'd been off my game. I mean, I thought I worked hard and did my best, but I got tired and restless just like anyone else.

"Mo?" I asked, once the other girls had moved toward the lockers.

She looked at me, not blinking as I tried to figure out how to word my question without sounding too insane. *What is in the envelope?!?!?*

"I'll probably have to read some of this stuff to my parents, since their English isn't so good," I said, and immediately felt guilty. It was true that my parents had defected from Romania before I was born; but they'd taught themselves English by watching daytime television and reading newspapers, and they were proud of the way they'd made a life for themselves here. Sometimes there were still things I needed to explain or help them with, but if it weren't for their accents they could have passed for having been born in this country.

"Okay," Mo said. "You can read to them."

"So it's not . . . secret or anything?"

"No, Noelle. It's not bad." One corner of her mouth pulled up, and I blushed. Of course she would know exactly what I was trying to get at. "It's just information about competition—boring, grown-up information, like flight to Philadelphia and leotards and money and itinerary. You don't need to worry."

The weight in my chest lifted, but only for a second, as Mo walked away, and then it settled in deeper than before. At least if I had been in trouble, I could have done something to fix it, like work harder, or apologize. But this was something I couldn't fix. Mo's words echoed in my brain—*flights, leotards, money*—and suddenly, my dream of the National Championships seemed impossible.

To go to that training camp with Coach Piserchia, my parents had had to take out a second mortgage on the building that housed both our home and our family's business. They'd made such an investment already I didn't know if I could ask them to make another one so soon. Then again, everything we'd put into gymnastics so far wouldn't have been worth much if I didn't take it all the way.

I tried to take a deep breath and visualize myself grabbing for that high bar that represented my dreams, feeling the smooth wood as I wrapped my fingers securely around the bar. But for some reason, whenever I got to that part, I could only imagine brushing it with my fingertips, close enough to leave marks in the chalk, but not close enough to stop myself from falling.